THE NEW ROAD TO KAILASH

SANDEEP MEHRA

BLUEROSE PUBLISHERS
India | U.K.

Copyright © Sandeep Mehra 2024

All rights reserved by author. No part of this publication may be reproduced, stored in a retrieval system or transmitted in any form or by any means, electronic, mechanical, photocopying, recording or otherwise, without the prior permission of the author. Although every precaution has been taken to verify the accuracy of the information contained herein, the publisher assume no responsibility for any errors or omissions. No liability is assumed for damages that may result from the use of information contained within.

BlueRose Publishers takes no responsibility for any damages, losses, or liabilities that may arise from the use or misuse of the information, products, or services provided in this publication.

For permissions requests or inquiries regarding this publication, please contact:

BLUEROSE PUBLISHERS
www.BlueRoseONE.com
info@bluerosepublishers.com
+91 8882 898 898
+4407342408967

ISBN: 978-93-6261-945-7

Cover design: Tahira
Typesetting: Tanya Raj Upadhyay

First Edition: July 2024

With the New Road to Kailash, there was hope for an Independent Tibet and secure Indian borders.

THE NEW ROAD TO KAILASH

Vasudhaiva Kutumbakam
The new Road to Kailash,
The new road to prosperity.

The Path to Heaven - Mount Kailash

In Sanatan Dharma, **Mount Kailash** *is recognized as the abode of Lord Shiva, who resides there, along with his consort goddess Parvati and their children, Ganesha and Kartikeya. As per the Hindu belief, Kailash is the Mount Meru, which is considered to be the stairway to heaven.*

Till date, it has been impossible for humans to climb Mount Kailash. It is the abode of Cosmic Energy, believed to be divine.

Kailash, once part of India, now Indians have to request for a Visa from Chinese authorities, as the region was encroached by China along with Tibet, in 1960. A wider majority of Indians dream to visit their sacred pilgrimage but are denied entry by China.

This tale follows a determined group of young individuals from India and its neighboring countries on a mission to restore balance and enhance quality of life in the region.

This was to fight debt traps, disease, disaster, and deceitful economic supremacy and allow the countries to live as per their free will.

The narrative also highlights the liberation of Tibet, allowing India to reclaim land and establish a buffer zone between them and China, leading to a reduction in defense spending.

Most importantly, Indians can now visit the sacred Kailash Mansarovar without any obstacles hindering their pilgrimage.

This book is a work of pure imagination. It is crafted to captivate and inspire; it draws inspiration from some real events and individuals but does not seek to portray them in a positive or negative light.

Dedication

This book draws its inspiration from the unsung heroes of modern India, the nameless soldiers who toil behind the scenes, sacrificing their personal lives for the greater good.

It also pays tribute to the Indian government, which has uplifted its citizens, fortified the armed forces, built world-class infrastructure, and fostered a thriving economy. Today, India stands tall, ready to boldly confront any form of global intimidation.

Moreover, the book finds inspiration in His Holiness Dalai Lama and the countless Tibetans who have been uprooted from their homes and forced into exile, yearning to return to their homeland.

It is my hope that this book will offer them a glimmer of hope towards an independent and economically prosper Tibet.

Acknowledgments

I would like to convey my heartfelt gratitude to **Mr. Rajan Pental**, who has not only supported and promoted my first book, *"The Rogue Bankers – Scam of 2001"*, but has also motivated me to complete this book, every time we meet. The book would not have been possible without Mr. Pental's encouragement.

This book is also the result of unending discussions I had with my wife **Sangeeta Mehra,** and sons **Chaitanya and Apurv**, on Indian History, culture, and Religion.

The idea which germinated in this fiction is a result of all those discussions we had.

I am thankful to Apurv, Chaitanya and Sangeeta for their input and editing this book.

Prologue

September 2029 marked a momentous occasion in my life. The day had finally arrived for Yang and me to exchange our vows in Dadong, her ancestral village near Pangzhutan, Lhasa, Tibet.

It was after a gap of almost seven decades, Tibet regained its original name, reclaiming its identity from the Chinese who had named it Xizang after invading it in 1960. While the locals referred to it as the "autonomous region of Tibet," China continued to use the name Xizang for official purposes.

Despite some believing that Tibet had become an extension of India after gaining independence, the truth was that Tibet stood as an independent nation with complete autonomy, supported by the Indian government.

A significant presence at our wedding was His Holiness, the Tibetan spiritual leader, who stayed in exile in India, between 1960 and 2028. He had returned to Lhasa the previous year. At 91 years old, he still appeared vibrant and full of life.

Yang had made a special request to him, to give herself away as the bride, a request that His Holiness could not refuse. There was a unique bond between Yang and His

Holiness, a connection that only a few knew. This bond had been forged over the course of 15 years.

The three-day wedding celebration was a mesmerizing fusion of spirituality and culture. Set against the breathtaking backdrop of the Himalayan landscapes, the ceremonies were conducted in accordance with the rich customs, rituals, and beliefs of the Tibetan people, making our wedding a truly unforgettable and distinctive experience.

As per the Tibetan tradition, parents had the responsibility of raising and arranging marriages for their children, and the children had the obligation to obey and honor their parents. When finding a bride or groom, the children had no right to inquire, especially women, who often went to their husbands' homes without even knowing what their husbands looked like.

In our case it was different. Both Yang and I had lost our parents, in the service of our respective nations. So, with the blessings of his holiness, the conservative villagers allowed Yang to not only select a groom for herself, but also marry an Indian.

This was the first of its kind marriage in Tibet, after it became an independent state again. The date of marriage was chosen by his holiness as 17th of September. Yang and I, both being orphans, his holiness had promised her to perform all traditional ceremonies, as Yang's father would have done.

For me, my brother and his family were to perform the ceremonies, while a whole lot of my relatives had specially flown to Lhasa, to enjoy the ceremonies. The village had no hotels, but as this wedding involved the presence of his holiness, some 30 rooms in Twang Monastery, were cleaned, painted and special arrangements were made to sleep the groom's family. Staff from Kang ding Hotel in Lhasa were brought here, to serve the guests.

His Holiness lived in Pelota Palace in Lhasa, which was some three hours' drive from Dadong. For the final marriage ceremony, the arrangements were made in the palace itself.

The ceremonies started on 15th, with my brother and his wife offering the bride's wedding dress and ornaments, to Yang. As per Tibetan tradition, the dress was supposed to be offered by my parents. As both my parents were no more, my brother assumed this responsibility. The bride was to wear this dress on the wedding day.

There was a feast for the entire village and guests, which followed this ceremony. Next day, the engagement ceremony was performed, followed by another feast. For the final wedding rituals, we travelled to Lhasa on 17th where his holiness was to give away Yang to me, post the ceremonies.

My brother and the relatives were surprised when came to know about His Holiness escorting the bride. I was able to convince them about Yang's some relation with

His Holiness. The challenge I faced, when they saw Indian Prime Minister at our reception. I had no explanation for the reason for his presence. It had to remain a secret.

The wedding pavilion was created in the extensive lawns of the palace. The palace had been abandoned since 1960s, when his Holiness migrated to India. On his return last year, the Palace was cleaned, painted, and redecorated and once again it became livable. This was the first marriage at Pelota Palace in a long time. In fact, no one on the guests list or the palace workers could remember anything like this at this place.

There were many relatives from my side, whom I had never met. There were some whom I was meeting after a gap of some 15 years. Many had last seen me during my parents' funeral.

What a day that was. My destiny was re-written, because of that day.

Preface

India was the most advanced civilization, much prior to the western world learned to cover itself.

India's journey of advancement began approximately in 1500 BCE during the Vedic era. This period marked the presence of remarkable intellectual, political, and cultural growth. It was a time of deep spiritual and intellectual exploration. The four Vedas - Rigveda, Samaveda, Yajurveda, and Atharvaveda, were the foundational texts of society, encompassing hymns, rituals, and philosophical discussions. These texts not only served as religious scriptures but also contained valuable scientific knowledge in fields like astronomy, mathematics, and medicine.

By the 7th century BC, India had founded structured education system and had established universities like Takshshila (Taxila) and Nalanda. The universities started attracting students from various countries. The curriculum included subjects like grammar, philosophy, medicine, archery, and astronomy. Scholars like Chanakya and Panini were associated with Takshashila.

Nalanda, a residential university could accommodate over 10,000 students, it had a vast library and offered advanced education in Buddhist philosophy, logic, mathematics, and linguistics. While the universities attracted education enthusiasts around the world, India's riches attracted invaders.

During the Golden Era of The Maurya Empire, led by Chandragupta Maurya and Chanakya, a highly efficient administration was established. The empire thrived, expanding its borders from the Hindu Kush in the northwest to Bengal in the east, and from the Himalayas in the north to the Deccan Plateau in the south.

Ashoka the Great, a prominent ruler of the Maurya dynasty, ruled from 268 to 232 BCE. Initially a fierce warrior, Ashoka underwent a significant transformation after the Kalinga War. He adopted Buddhism and committed himself to non-violence, compassion, and moral law (Dharma). Ashoka's reign saw notable advancements in infrastructure, such as the construction of roads, hospitals, and irrigation systems. Additionally, he played a crucial role in spreading Buddhism throughout Asia by sending missionaries to distant lands like Sri Lanka, Central Asia, and Southeast Asia.

However, following Ashoka's death, the decline of the Maurya Empire began. Subsequent rulers struggled to maintain the same level of control and stability, leading to internal conflicts and fragmentation. Also, some believe that practice of Non-violence is never good for a country, if it surrenders at the time of war.

The gradual decline in the power of the empire, finally ended in 187 BCE with the death of the seventh decedent of Ashoka, who was named *Brihadratha*.

Brihadratha was killed by his own general, Pushpamitra Shunga, who laid the foundation of Shunga Empire. Pushpamitra had taken help of the Chinese tribal leader Shih Huangdi, to establish the Shunga Empire. Shih, in turn, back stabbed Pushpamitra to separate large portion of lands and established the Quin Empire, known as China.

It is believed that while historically this entire piece of land belonged to India, it never came back. The land included the place encompassing the mighty and sacred Kailash Mansarovar, the Hindu Pilgrimage.

Gradually, as India continued to practice Non-Violence, this benefitted the foreign invaders, who, having no knowledge or wealth of their own, knew nothing, but invasion and war.

There are two ways of establishing your supremacy. One, raise your standards and be superior, and the other, bring down the one greater than you, to your level or lower than your level. As the invaders could not accept the Indian knowledge supremacy, they took it on themselves to destroy these knowledge hubs.

When Taxila university was burnt by the Persian invaders, Huns, they destroyed the knowledge, which was created over generations. The Persians had no literal match with Indian sages, so they killed them, in order to bring the world knowledge to the level of their own.

Similarly, when Bakhtiyar Khilji invaded, he burnt Nalanda university. The library of the university was so vast that it continued to burn for many months.

Like India, China too saw a division of empire. In the 6th century AD, Yarlung Kings established a large empire, and named it Tibet. The religion was Buddhism, which continued since the Mauryan Empire, and is continued till present day. During the same period, another kingdom was established around Mount Kailash, called Zhangzhung, which practiced Bon religion, which was again similar to Buddhism.

By the end of the 8th century, the Tibetan empire reached its greatest extent. In 1244, Kublai Khan conquered Tibet and included it into the Mongol Empire. By 1271, the Mongols realized that this barren piece of land was a continuous cost to their kingdom, hence declared autonomy for Tibet, allowing them to fend for themselves. Now, Tibet was ruled by the spiritual leaders, who are called Lamas.

Tibet continued to be ruled by spiritual leaders till 1960, when it was conquered by China and included into the vast piece of Chinese controlled land. By 1965, the Chinese also realized, that Tibet is a financial burden on the Chinese economy and declared it as an autonomous region but continued with contributing for its upkeep.

The lands were barren. With limited cultivable land, livestock raising was the primary occupation on the Tibetan Plateau. The limited crops and livestock were not sufficient for the population, hence China always had to contribute immensely, towards Tibetan's upkeep. Still, China wanted control of Tibet, as because of Tibet, it had direct access to India and Pakistan.

Because of this direct access, India had to spend billions for securing its borders from hostile China.

With the New Road to Kailash, there was hope for an Independent Tibet and secure Indian borders.

Table of Contents

Dedication .... *vii*
Acknowledgments .... *viii*
Prologue .... *ix*
Preface .... *xiii*
The Declaration 1
Adwait 6
Yang 11
Shoelace 24
The student 31
The business 35
Beginning the cause 41
The Cop 49
Commando 62
The Prince 82
Meeting The Prince 90
The agency 104
Ranjit Singh 117
Jon Russel 161
Forming the Team 178
The Revenge 188
The new India 205

Wang	211
The Conflict	216
Ismail and Faridah	226
Kashgar	233
The Independence	242
The Reply	247

CHAPTER 01

The Declaration

June 18, 2013. The G9 summit, concluded in Brussels, Belgium.

The G9 or Group of nine nations meets every year and is considered to be an elitist group. It consists of participation by heads of state of Canada, France, Germany, Italy, Japan, Netherlands, Sweden, United Kingdom, and United States.

During the closure address, the G9 President Ursula Stevenson concluded the discussions by stating:

"The strategies and measures were needed to combat China's growing economic dominance".

Her speech underscored the importance of a unified and strategic approach to ensure a balanced and fair global economic landscape.

President Stevenson emphasized the urgent need for transparent and equitable trade practices. She highlighted issues such as state subsidies and non-tariff barriers imposed by China, which distort global trade. She advocated for the modernization of the World Trade

Organization (WTO) to better handle contemporary trade challenges and to enforce fair practices more effectively. Stevenson also called for increased investment in research and development to maintain technological leadership in critical fields such as artificial intelligence, 5G, and biotechnology. She underscored the importance of robust cybersecurity measures to protect intellectual property and sensitive data from cyber threats linked to Chinese entities.

The president encouraged strategic partnerships with other nations towards increased investments in global infrastructure projects to provide alternatives to China's Belt and Road Initiative (BRI). These projects should adhere to high standards of transparency and sustainability unlike China, she stated. By now, it was understood that BRI was aimed by China, towards global encroachment.

"Time has come, to identify a leader to check the unchecked economic growth of China, which could be from a neighboring country to China. This country should serve as an alternative to China, without having any expansionist ambitions, and should be a supportive nation."

India.

The glory which India had lost due to multiple invasions and colonization, started coming back during the second decade of the 21st century. This was when, India embarked on an ambitious journey to enhance various aspects such as strengthening of economy, enhanced security inviting investments, improving infrastructure and roads, and ensuring border security. These efforts now reflect India's commitment to the safety, prosperity, and technological advancement of its citizens.

By now, the heads of major Global companies were Indians and soon the heads of two world powers were also Indians.

India's defense and security sectors underwent significant upgrades to modernize the armed forces and safeguard national security. The "Make in India" initiative encouraged domestic manufacturing of defense equipment, reducing dependence on imports and fostering innovation. The introduction of advanced fighter jets, the development of indigenous missiles, and the commissioning of stealth frigates and submarines greatly enhanced India's military capabilities.

India also pioneered substantial investments in digital payment networks, which helped immediate payments to the remotest beneficiary, helping Indian business and in turn, economy to grow.

India also placed great emphasis on infrastructure development and the improvement of roads. This includes the construction and maintenance of robust road networks, facilitating smoother transportation and connectivity across the nation.

The efforts are to bring back the lost glory of India.

Soon after the G9 summit, Ralph Stevens, the CIA chief approached Prince. It was time to curtail China's expansionism.

Still there had to be a lead country leader for the project. The leader had to be from a neighboring country. Taiwan, Vietnam, Mongolia, South Korea were out of question. India again was under a corrupt dynastic rule and a lame leader.

Prince, who was half Indian and Half British, chose Pakistan and started the project. But soon, Price was stuck as Pakistan believed in destructions, this was not what the G9 wanted. Pakistan also had their own agenda with China due to fundamentalism, which had nothing to do with G9.

An opportunity arose when the Indians toppled the dynastic rule and chose a leader from a modest upbringing. This leader had a flawless tenure as a head of an Indian state for over a decade.

Despite India not being part of the G9, the Indian Prime Minister was extended invitations to the G9 summits, hence forth.

During the 2015 summit, India introduced a unique approach to the G9. While the western countries preferred their conventional, economic exploitation based method, India proposed a peaceful, advantageous and development-based approach to address the current issues.

The strategy introduced by India focused on advancement, aiming to benefit prosperous as well as economically disadvantaged nations, to secure economic independence. Additionally, there was a strategy in place to minimize military tensions in the area by clearly defining borders. This would ultimately lead to a reduction in defense spending, allowing funds to be redirected towards improving the lives of the people.

As a result, in the 2015 summit, two distinct approaches emerged towards a shared objective. One led by the west and the other by India.

The first approach was to be led by CIA, while the second which was development based, by India. The western approach was named as Project Wall, while the Indian, *Brihadratha*, after the last Mauryan emperor.

Back home, the Indian Prime minister made it clear to the National Security Advisor (NSA) Ranjit Singh that he wants a permanent solution to all the border conflicts. The solution should be development based and the violence should only be used in select, extreme cases.

The NSA selected his core team. There was an advantage for India, as taking shelter behind the infrastructure and other developments, India started cementing its position and position of its neighboring countries, permanently.

This is when *Emperor Brihadratha* was reborn.

CHAPTER

Adwait

My name is Adwait Sharma, and I am an ex-national swimmer from India. I met Yang for the first time in 2009, at Talkatora Swimming pool in New Delhi.

I was in the National swimming team and was practicing for the 2010 Commonwealth games, which were to be held in New Delhi next year.

It was early December of year 2009. While the entire New Delhi was shivering in cold wave, the swimming pool complex was temperature controlled at 27□C. After the first jump in the pool, gradually our bodies used to adapt to the temperature.

This swimming pool was constructed for the year 1982 Asian Games. While the pool continued to be used for practice since then, it was renovated for the Commonwealth games by adding a roof on the structure, which reflected roman architecture.

I am a third-generation swimmer in my family. My grandfather participated in the first Asian games in New Delhi, in the year 1951. Then my father in the ninth Asian games, again in New Delhi in 1982 and thereafter in many international swimming events. Now, it was my turn.

I had completed my four-hour morning practice schedule and was leaving the pool for college when I first saw Yang. She was walking along with Ms. Dolma.

Ms. Dolma was our swimming sensation from the 9th Asian games, 1982 and was a close friend to my dad. She was a well-respected swimmer, who participated in various international swimming events and was now a trainer for Indian team.

Due to her Northeastern features, I presumed Yang to be relative of Ms. Dolma. She had a bony structure, was very fair, Mongolian eyes and hair like silk. Eyes had sincerity, she smiled self-consciously, and that was what attracted me towards her.

Ms. Dolma was chatting endlessly with Mr. Subramaniam, chief coach for the Indian team. My steps towards the exit became slower and slower. I could not miss the opportunity, to at least get introduced to the beauty. And knowing Ms. Dolma, I was sure, I'll be introduced.

My luck smiled, Mr. Subramaniam attended a phone call over his hand phone and the chatter stopped. Finding some time, I wished Ms. Dolma, good morning, and stopped a little longer.

"Kaisa hai Handsome" (how are you handsome), Ms. Dolma enquired in her usual energetic tone.

I responded Ms. Dolma with 'all good mam'.

Of course, I was the lead Indian swimmer and enjoyed all the attention. Ms. Dolma's experienced eyes did not miss that my gaze was stuck to the Northeastern beauty. Ms. Dolma was ever obliging, and here again, she introduced Yang, as her niece.

A polite and brief handshake was all I needed for the day.

When I got that, Ms. Dolma enquired if I was going to college. If I was, I could drop Yang to the Tibetan monastery area.

I would have been a fool if I had said no.

Well, I never needed any attendance in the college. Being a National swimmer, attendance, free meals in the college café, a celebrity status, was all part of life for me. I was most regular to my college, but the reason was not studies, but free meals and attention. Today, the added reason was Yang.

I was totally smitten with the beauty and had to go to college for her. Hardeep, who was the regular pillion on my motorbike, had to catch the DTC bus that day. He was most understanding.

On way to the motorbike parking, I wanted to know about her.

She said that she stayed in Tibetan Monastery area and studied Political Science in Jesus & Merry College. She was in the first year of her graduation. I was in my final year in Hindu College.

Yang told me, she had stayed the night with her aunt Dolma and had to go home, before attending a late evening presentation on Tibet, that day. While studying, she had joined the Tibetan liberation movement and was taking active part in the cause. I had no idea about the movement.

She and her aunt Dolma were close. Today, she had this free time and hence wanted to see the swimming pool complex. She planned to go home along with Aunt Dolma, but as there was some change in plans, she was *'bothering'* me.

What to tell, this was the best *'botheration'*, I could ever get in my life.

Monastery was not exactly on my way to the college; however, I didn't mind. The distance to monastery was just 12 KMs, but I took full one hour to cover that.

When I asked for her number while dropping her off, she said she was seeing someone and sharing of number was not appropriate.

I had developed a somewhat ego, for all the achievements in such younger age and, for my North Indian looks. You can imagine, what a prick it was on the balloon of my thoughts. This anti-climax was not what I was expecting.

I was somewhat sad during the remaining drive to my college. But, once I reached it, I was my cheery self once again.

In this life, you never know whom you would meet, when and under what circumstances.

It was not until seven years; I saw Yang next. That too, some 6,000 KMs away from Delhi, and under totally different circumstance.

We were destined to meet.

CHAPTER 03

Yang

Yangchen Rgya Mtsho, addressed as Yang by people close to her, was born in Dadong village, which is considered to be the most beautiful village near Lhasa, the stunning capital of Tibet. Yang possessed extraordinary beauty and intelligence.

Born into a family deeply rooted in Tibetan culture and resistance, Yang grew up hearing stories of her ancestors' bravery and their unwavering commitment to Tibet's independence. Inspired by their legacy, she felt a strong calling to follow in their footsteps and to contribute towards the cause.

From an early age, Yang displayed exceptional skills in observation, deduction, and disguise. Her parents, recognizing her unique abilities, decided to enroll her in a secret underground organization, Tibetan Resistance Movement or TRM, which is dedicated to freeing Tibet from Chinese oppression.

She was barely sixteen years of age. Under the guidance of seasoned resistance fighters, Yang honed her skills as an operative. Within a year of training in Lhasa, Yang was ready to be the youngest agent in the history of spy world.

With her captivating beauty and charming personality, Yang could seamlessly blend into Chinese society, gaining access to valuable information.

She learned Mandarin fluently and also various other professional skills. She learnt the work of an electrician, telephone and television mechanic, plumber, she could also drive well. All this helped her to assume different roles to get inside information.

She used her intelligence-gathering skills to gather classified information and relay it back to TRM. Her reports proved instrumental and helped TRM in strategizing and planning future operations.

Over the next three years, Yang became an indispensable asset to TRM. Her bravery and determination were unwavering, even in the face of danger. She risked her life on multiple occasions to obtain vital intelligence, always keeping the bigger picture in mind — freeing Tibet from Chinese control.

As an operative, she would travel to Beijing, and other parts of China. She would find some employment, which would be a cover, to collect information around various Chinese projects.

She will see to it that she selects some lowly paying jobs. The low jobs would ensure, she is never under radar. It would also give her the flexibility of being in places which could be sensitive, holding secret information or were conduit to getting secret information.

The first job she took was as a security guard at the parking lot of the National Peoples' Congress building. While the actual building was guarded by highly trained security teams, the car park was left with private security agencies.

Here, she befriended a few drivers of the politicians. Having a keen eye, she started analyzing, which politician could be of much help. Identifying the right ones, she came in contact with the drivers and slipped some tiny electronic bugs into their clothes, hats or even cars, wherever she could get access. Now, TRM would get a continuous stream of information, whatever would be discussed inside the car.

She learnt that China had come to know about an uprising near Lhasa.

Thanks to a bug in the defense secretary's car, Yang could get a whiff of discussion of military strategy to be used to suppress that uprising. She swiftly transmitted the information to the TRM headquarters, who used it to reorganize their large-scale operation to reclaim their homeland.

This operation was meticulously planned and executed, catching the Chinese forces off-guard.

The Tibetan resistance fighters, armed with the knowledge provided by Yang, engaged in a fierce battle with the Chinese military. The people of Tibet, inspired by the courage and determination of the resistance, rose in support.

This was in 2008 and is seen as the first organized independence movement of Tibet.

Within a week, the government informers, who had informed the uprising to the government agency, went missing, never to be found. The change of location was considered as their failure by the Chinese government, and they had to pay for it with their lives.

Slowly, Yang modified her operations. She was beautiful, and when dressed right, she could be a stunner.

She changed her strategy and instead of lying low, she started attending various conferences and started mingling with influential Chinese figures as an arm candy. Most Chinese officials came to the parties with their mistresses. Yang started being in high demand.

Meeting the influential, she discovered a growing dissatisfaction among certain officials regarding the Chinese government's policies. The dissatisfaction was also regarding policies on Tibet. She capitalized on this opportunity and whenever she met someone important, tried to sway the discussion towards the Tibetan cause, ensuring never to raise any suspicion.

She would use all techniques to be closer to the politicians and ensure she is invited to formal gatherings as well.

During a chanced meeting with a Chinese Minister of Technology, Yang came to know about operation *Shoelace*.

The minister was coordinating this operation, wherein the best Chinese hackers were competing. The competition was being held in Hotel Peninsula, Beijing, where the minister was staying. What the minister had not told anyone, *shoelace* was aimed to hack into the SWIFT payment system of the USA.

Yang subtly persuaded the minister for drinks and when he was drunk, accompanied him to his room. Some more drinks and then the minister started blabbering everything about *shoelace*, in drunken state.

Of late, Chinese Government was facing stiff challenges over finance. While the business was good and the economy booming, the government policy mandated parking of foreign currency, in foreign countries only, investing for hostile takeovers. A large sum was needed back home, for keeping dissidents in place and for many covert operations. For instance, maintaining Tibet and Mongolia needed money.

So, when the minister of technology suggested operation *Shoelace*, the majority was thrilled.

Knowing about this operation, Yang decided to use this for the cause of Tibet. She found out there were seven finalists. One amongst them was to be used by the Government for the operation. It was a one-man job. That one was chosen and the remaining six were let go.

Yang befriended Ming, who could not make it to the final and was returning home by train. Yang planned quickly and was on the train as well.

While Ming was sad for losing, he was thrilled when a beauty like Yang chose a seat next to him, on the 11 hours long train journey.

And when Yang initiated the talk, his heart skipped a beat.

Yang introduced herself as a second-generation Chinese American citizen, working as CEO of her father's startup engineering company in the USA. She was presently visiting her grandparents in China. She had taken a flight to Beijing and now was on the train towards her village.

The chatter continued; Yang kept appreciating everything Ming was saying. Having not experienced this kind of attention, and that too from a successful beauty, Ming continued talking about his abilities as a hacker. He was cautious though, not to speak about his recent experience at the government project.

They were travelling through Beijing – Kunming high speed train, which covered 2,700 KMs in just over 14 hours. Ming was travelling till Changsha, which is around 1,500 KMs from Beijing. Yang was cautious and not knowing earlier the destination for Ming, had purchased the ticket till last stop, which leads to the Mountain town of Deqin.

Halfway through the journey, Yang asked him, if he would like to visit her village in Deqin. Smitten with her beauty, Ming could not say no.

Ming was living with his parents in Changsha. His parents knew that he was returning. So, he called them to inform them that he would be delayed by a few days, as some business opportunity had come up.

Not entirely a lie, as during discussion, Yang had hinted him a job of his liking, in the USA.

By now, Ming felt quite comfortable with Yang and had found a different type of confidence, due to receptiveness of Yang. All the doubts, as why this beauty was interested in him, vanished, when she said that she had clubbed her holiday with business and planned to hire talented fellow Chinese.

Deqin is a Tibetan Mountain Getaway, which is an alpine Tibetan town about 6 hours' drive from Kunming. It is at 3,600 meters elevation, hence, there is very little inhabitancy here.

Considering Yang was visiting her grandparents in a small town, they both decided to stay separately. Yang stayed at a homestay claiming to be her grandparents' home. The homestay was arranged by one of her TRM contacts. Ming was placed by Yang's contact in a motel. This contact had also arranged unlimited supply of Chhang (Tibetan rice wine) for Ming, while Yang promised a visit during the night.

On the second night, Yang asked about the work Ming was supposed to execute in Beijing. Ming could not restrain and told her everything about project Shoelace. Yang acted surprized and asked him if he could actually do this type of hacking.

He said, the ask from the government was different, but he has his own way of doing this, which is even better than, what government proposed.

Ming continued, "for this, I need a mail ID of anyone within a bank. I would place a virus in an attachment on the mail and send it to that mail ID. Once the attachment would be opened, the virus would find its way into the banking system and track the person who had the authority to make funds transfers. The virus will also find the IDs and passwords used for the electronic payments. Once that is known, making an electronic bank transfer would be a child's play".

Yang had a question, "why the virus will not be detected by the Bank's firewalls?" Ming replied, he could encrypt the virus with the highest, 256 bits encryption, which normal firewalls cannot detect. And the virus attack would be on a lower cyber capable bank, where cyber security is laxed.

"If you could do that, I will marry you", Yang said, out of nowhere.

She told him, she had a few friends in the banking and can get him the desired mail ID. If he succeeds, they will never have to worry about finances anymore. She, being an American citizen, can take her husband to the USA and then, they can settle down in some remote island.

Ming was concerned, as the act was illegal. Earlier, he was supposed to perform this through the government systems, so he could be saved. But now, on his own, this was dangerous, as the technology ministry was aware about his capabilities.

Yang told him not to worry. The detection will take at least a week, by when, they would be in America, without a trace. She will get his documentation started and they can elope the next day of the hack.

Henceforth, Ming couldn't see anything better than the idea of elopement and good life with this beauty.

The mail ID was provided by Yang the next day. The ID belonged to a staff in Bangladesh Islamic Bank. This bank was a safer bet, due to laxed Cyber security.

Another advantage of choosing a bank in Bangladesh was, here, the banks were closed on Fridays and Saturdays, while in most other countries, they were closed on Saturdays and Sundays.

When they would perform their act, they could do that on a Thursday night. It would not be detected till Sunday. As on Sundays, other banks are closed, they would get full 72 hours to transfer the monies electronically to different locations.

Ming created a mutable tracer virus and attached it to the mail attachment, titled 'tax refund'. This mail he sent the next day.

Within weeks, the world was shocked with the news of USD fifty million SWIFT hack in Bangladesh Islamic Bank. The money was siphoned off through casinos of Fiji, Mauritius, and far-flung countries. This money was never received back by the Bank.

The virus did its trick. Once the mail was seen by the recipient, he got curious to see the title "tax refund". The gullible employee opened the attachment, to find nothing on it, so closed it.

The virus was already on its way, the moment the attachment was opened. For full one week, the virus kept scanning the mailboxes to find the staff who could make funds transfers. When that was found, it transferred itself to that staff's computer.

A wait for another day, and the virus sent an alert to Ming, who could see the live screen of the employee. Ming could also get control of the computer remotely, through the virus.

The login ID was visible on the screen. Ming kept keying in the wrong password to get the account locked. Once the account was locked, the employee was supposed to get the account unlocked. Ming remotely switched on "show password" toggle. The new password was now visible on the screen.

They waited for another week and then came into action for funds transfers on next Friday.

First the money went to a casino's account in some far-flung islands in Fiji, from where it went to Mongolia, then Sri Lanka, and Vietnam. In Vietnam, the money was cashed through different accounts, redeposited in another account and then it was transferred to some 250+ accounts managed by Tibetan people. The accounts were in different countries, so escaped Chinese surveillance. At every step, the money was layered in such a way that it mixed with other monies in the accounts, hence it lost its identity.

The greater shock was for the Chinese authorities managing operation Shoelace. While others within the government, knowing about the operation congratulated them for the successful operation, they were the ones having no clue about this.

When it was known to be an outsider's job, they tried to trace all the seven finalists to scan their computers. Only six could be found with Ming, missing. His parents were taken into custody.

They kept repeating that he never returned from Beijing. They told the authorities about the phone call, wherein he had informed them about his delayed return and getting some assignment. They further informed the authorities that he continued calling them till a few days ago.

The authorities checked phone logs and found the calls between his parents and him, the last location was seen as Deqin.

The Police reached Deqin. Where Ming was reported as missing by the motel staff for the last two days. The staff also gave a description of a pretty girl visiting him. There was no record of that girl, and no one knew her. The motel was not equipped with CCTV, so the police had to base their investigation on the provided description.

Ming's laptop was found intact in his room. This was taken into custody along with his belongings by the police. The laptop had a damaged hard drive, so was of no help.

Ming was never found, as his body was left deep in a cave, which was full of rodents. Yang was already in Beijing by then, in her Beijing avatar.

This money was the best gift, Yang could provide for the Tibetan movement. Thankfully, she was in disguise during the train journey and while in Deqin. Even though the train had CCTV footage, she could not be placed.

This episode, along with frequent leaking of information did not go unnoticed with the Chinese authorities. They became increasingly suspicious that there was someone getting the information in advance. When the Chinese Minister of Technology was found dead, Yang was advised by her superiors to shift base.

She left Beijing, came to Lhasa, then through the mountains into Ladakh. Having stayed in Ladakh for a few weeks, she again shifted her base to New Delhi.

This was December 2009. This is when Yang first met with Adwait at Talkatora Swimming pool.

CHAPTER

Shoelace

Fang Gonxha, the minister of technology was summoned by Wang, the Chinese Vice President to his office. After the news of Bangladesh Banks's SWIFT hack came out, Wang had called Gonxha to congratulate him for the success.

Fang had spent the weekend with his new girlfriend, so was not able to catch up with his team. He never wanted to act surprised, so thanked the Vice President for the good wishes and for showing faith in him.

It was only after an hour, when his deputy was finally able to reach him, to let him know that they were screwed.

As the news of him and his team getting screwed reached the higher circles, the Vice President summoned him again. This time the tone was not that pleasant, and the discussion was short.

Wang: Fashengle Shenme? (What Happened)

Fang: Woen zhengzai diaocha xisansheng (we are investigating sir)

Wang: Ni renwei zhe shi shibai ma he xie dai moduan shoelace? (Do you see this as your failure and end to shoelace)

Fang: Yidian ye bu xisanshen. Woen hui zai qita yinhang qude Chenggong. (Not at all sir. We will succeed in other banks)

Wang: Kan dao ni chenggongle. Huozhe ni zoule. (See you succeed. Or you are gone)

Fang was dismissed. He knew very well that he had to succeed at other banks, or this would be an end to his political career.

In his dream that night, he saw his body floating in a large Lake. He was later shifted to his official quarters in Beijing in his dream.

The threat was looming. Fang was in double minds, should he initiate Shoelace immediately or should wait.

Waiting made more sense, as at present, the world banks and SWIFT management were on their toes. Their alertness could put the plans in jeopardy.

Also, the more he delays, the more time he would have politically, if his team fails. So, he waited for about two months.

Prabhakar worked with Columbia Commercial Bank in Mumbai as head of fraud monitoring. One fine morning at about 08:30, he received a call on his hand phone, from an unknown number. The initial digits suggested the call from Thailand.

Considering it to be a spam call, Prabhakar disconnected. The call came again. On the third time, he picked up.

It was Abhisit Bolbarn, his counterpart from Bangkok. Abhisit was calling to inform that a few accounts in their Bangkok branch were receiving millions of dollars from India. There were further requests for the transfer of the received amount to different banks in different locations across Asia.

Abhisit enquired if there was any bank in India called Modern bank.

Modern was a schedule commercial bank in India, so, Prabhakar said, yes.

Abhisit shared that the money is from that bank and till now, some six inward remittances have been received for amounts between 6 to 7 million USD each. An equal amount has been requested electronically to be transferred to different accounts.

This was strange. Considering Modern Bank's operations, the transactions should ideally have been local. Also, transactions involving this big amount, could have been done at the branch and 08:30 AM was not the time, when the branches are usually open.

Prabhakar asked Abhisit if he can stall the onward remittances. Abhisit said that he can, but for a shorter period. If the stalling has to go beyond bank closure time,

Prabhakar had to share some orders from Indian Judiciary for the same.

There is a time gap between India and Thailand and Thailand is 1.5 hours ahead of India. Prabhakar still had some good time in hand.

But things can go wrong.

When Prabhakar contacted Sumit, head of Fraud Prevention of Modern bank, his immediate reaction was, nothing of this sort can happen at their bank, as they were secure. Still, he would review when he reached office.

Prabhakar reminded him about the recent SWIFT heist at Bangladesh Islamic Bank. Still Sumit was reluctant, but he promised to check.

At 10:30 India time, Prabhakar reminded Sumit about the issue, as Abhisit could no longer hold the funds without an approval from higherups.

Sumit said he had just reached the office and was walking towards his cabin; he will connect with the right business unit to check.

At 12:30, there was a frantic call from Sumit stating "dude, we have lost millions".

They had realized that some 340 crores of Indian Rupees, (45 million USD) had been transferred fraudulently to some undisclosed locations in Asia Pacific, early morning. They had no clue about these transactions. He requested Prabhakar for his help, restoring the money, even some partial recovery would do.

Now the problem was, it was already 12:30 in India and 02:00 PM in Thailand. The banks close in Thailand at 03:00 and before that, Modern bank had to get some sort of legal request from some Indian Law enforcement, to stall the funds.

Prabhakar had worked with Law enforcement, so he guided Sumit. Time was short, so he took charge.

Sumit got the complaint drafted on their bank's official stationery and got it signed from the authorized signatory.

That done, Prabhakar, then called the local police officer, who was an ex-colleague, and requested him to accept the complaint and put an acknowledging stamp on the receipt.

Prabhakar then asked Sumit for a Scanned copy of the acknowledgement. This was then shared with Abhisit over email.

It was already 04:00 PM in Thailand. Still, having received the lawful communication, Abhisit sent it for approvals of his business seniors and legal head. The legal head asked for an indemnity bond from Modern Bank but provided another day's time for this.

By the next evening all the money was safely returned to Modern Bank.

By 10:00 PM Chinese time, Fang was made aware by his subordinate, about another blow to Shoelace.

By 10:30, he sent a message to Wang.

By 10:45, there were three unmarked police vans at his residence. He was physically taken to the residence of Wang.

Fang pleaded for one more chance. Wang was a patient man, so it was granted.

Next month, the team Shoelace tried at Bank of Ceylon. The bank authorities were already alert, so team Shoelace failed again.

Next morning, when Fang was taking a bath, officials landed in his bathroom. They allowed him to dress, then escorted him to an unknown place.

On the seventh day, a highly decomposed body was found in Kunming Lake. While the official records declared it an unidentified body, people close to Fang knew this was him. It was the same as Fang's dream.

This is how China worked.

This was an exemplary punishment for showing laxity at work. Although, there was no fault of Fang, still he, being in charge of the project, was considered lax in controlling the information flow about the project, which lead to getting in hands of a competitor. The competitor used it, making it useless for any further utilization.

Still, there was no trace of that competitor.

The investigation revealed that Ming had not left China.

Where he was? No one could comment. As for the girl, the search was still on. Her description shared by the Motel staff was being matched with all the co passengers of Ming. She could be anywhere.

CHAPTER

The student

Although, she was already in her early twenties, Yang created a fake ID keeping the same name, which showed her as a nineteen-year-old Indian citizen. Because of her lean frame, extraordinary looks, and Mongolian features, no one could judge her actual age of twenty-four.

She got an admission in Jesus and Merry College, New Delhi, as an under grad. Because of some plastic surgery, she had higher cheek bones, wider forehead, and bigger bustline. Being a master of disguises, she always donned dark shades. With this, while she appeared to be classy, in fact she was avoiding all sorts of cameras, a few could be facial recognition ones.

Yang by now, was a highly trained operative. Her bosses in Lhasa had asked her to remain low, hence, she made sure whom she met.

Three years, she studied at Jesus & Merry college, she made sure she does not attract any unwarranted attention. Hence, she engrossed herself in studies only.

As per her new documents, she was born in St. Stephens Hospital in North Delhi, to a Tibetan couple, who worked near Tibetan monastery. Her mother ran a beauty parlor, while her father had a shop, selling woolen garments. She had two siblings, 17-year-old brother Ngawang and 14-year-old sister, Lhamo. They all lived in a small dwelling near Tibetan migrants' settlement on the banks of river Yamuna.

This settlement was started in the year 1959-60 for the Tibetan refugees who came to India along with their spiritual leader, after the occupation of Tibet by China. They all initially settled in Dharamshala in Himachal Pradesh. Later, the refugees were allotted land in New Delhi where the present-day settlement exists. They set up their refugee camp, on the Yamuna riverbed.

After the Sino-India War in 1962, many of the refugees who had previously settled temporarily near the Indo-Chinese border, also shifted here. Today, this place is home to the second generation of Tibet refugees and is also known as "Little-Tibet" or "Mini-Tibet".

There is a monastery, which is managed by the followers of Tibetan Spiritual leader. The monastery ensures education, career counselling and social welfare to the Tibetans. The ask by the monastery is one, follow your bloodline, marry within the community and be faithful to the leader.

So, when Adwait Sharma asked for her number, Yang's emotions were split.

Her heart wanted to share the number, make friends with Adwait and if all goes well, she could have a stable, peaceful life with this handsome, rich inheritor. Aunt Dolma knew Adwait's family and hence briefed Yang.

However, her brain guided the opposite. She had a past and had also promised to dedicate her life for the Tibetan cause. She could not afford to indulge in any sort of diversions.

Yang had planned to stay in New Delhi till she got a signal, that she was dropped from the lookout by the Chinese authorities. She had already enrolled for a three-year undergrad course. This, she calculated, was enough time to wait, and then she would decide on her next move.

She had enough money. While the money from the SWIFT hack was transferred to the TRM, they had given her a generous sum, to continue the good work.

Jesus & Merry College girls were known for having an active social life. Yang strictly avoided that. Her avoidance was to such an extent that she was often called an ice maiden by her classmates. No one could imagine why such a beauty would not enjoy life. No one could imagine Yang's past.

The college was on the South Delhi Campus and the area was full of wealthy lads, who made rounds of the college to find dates. The lads included cricketers, sons of Diplomats, Bureaucrats and Politicians. While the other girls looked their future husbands I them, Yang kept aloof.

These three years were her sabbatical. She had to return to the active operations life when the dust had settled. During these three years, she did nothing but studied. And in the free time helped Tibetan children finding the right path and making the world aware about Tibet and Tibetans.

CHAPTER 06

The business

In June 2010, I graduated from college. Belonging to a successful business family, I did not have to look for a job. It was understood that I would join my father's business.

My father owned a well-known brand of electrical home appliances. I joined him and immediately, was made in-charge of the production line. I was supposed to supervise the manufacturing.

Work timings suited me. My swimming practice started at 06:00 AM every day. Four-hour practice schedule ended by 10:00 and I could reach the factory by 10:30.

There was hardly anything for me to do at the factory. I stayed there till 02:30 PM and then left for the swimming pool for another four-hour practice session. That is what made my day in those days.

My daily routine had always been packed. Earlier, it was swimming – school – swimming and then home. Later, it was swimming – college – swimming and then home. Now it was swimming – factory – swimming, and home.

Whatever time was left from this, I used most of it to relax and prepare for the next day practice.

Although in my early twenties, I did not have any serious relationships. For one - there was no time for that, and two – the emotional drama irked me.

I had seen many of my friends, boys and girls being romantic "baby, I am missing you", baby - this, baby - that. Girls' and boys' public display of affection, marking their 'Territories", just like animals do. And then, when the territory was breached, their public display of emotions, shouting, crying.

I was not made for all this.

I had had some flings during school and college days, but they were more like infatuations, just to explore female anatomy. Being a swimmer, I was tall, tanned, and lean. My North Indian looks added to the personality, hence there was no dearth of interesting girls in my life. I always kept Saturday evenings free, for partying. On Saturdays, I could afford to be up till late at night, as there was no swimming practice on Sundays.

This was the time; I could explore more with girls too. No question of a serious relationship, as after some time, it bored me. I could never get attached to anyone. I called it a manufacturing defect in me. But it proved to be the best trait in the later part of my life.

Working at the factory was fun for the initial few weeks, but soon it became monotonous. The Commonwealth games were to be held in December. I had no choice but to continue like this till then. I had already made up my mind to do something else when the games were over. I could never live a static life. Having been raised as an independent individual, I wanted to remain that way. Never wanted to get tied up with anything. I knew my father would never subscribe to my idea of doing something else. But I was confident that I would be able to convince him.

Commonwealth games were over in December 2010. I missed the bronze medal in 200 Mts. Breaststroke event by 20 milli seconds. In 100Mts., I came 5th.

Although I did not win any medal for the country, I was offered a job in paramilitary forces of India. This was the opening I was looking for. I could continue with my passion, which was swimming. This also ensured a steady income for me, while I pursued my passion.

And, of course, I did not have to work at our factory. So, I said yes.

While saying 'yes', to the force's commander, offering me the job was easy, it was not that easy at my home.

My father, Mr. Anurag Sharma, wanted to retire early. He, had been a sportsman, excelling in swimming, diving, and athletics. He was also a qualified coach and international referee. He often planned to retire early and pursue his passion again, in coaching and refereeing.

He had confessed to me, going to the factory every day bored him too. But as this factory was passed on to him by his father, he had no other livelihood. My grandad was strict in his days, and in those days, Indian children had no say before their fathers. So, my father had no option.

Being at the swimming pool was fun. He could meet up with his old swimming friends, who were now coaches or swimming managers. He was a handsome man in his early days too. As Ms. Dolma had confided with me, he had great female fan following. All this, he missed working at the factory.

So, one could imagine his disappointment when I told him about my decision. My contention was that I never wanted to join him in business. Moreover, while my elder brother was already helping him in the business, I should be allowed to pursue my own career path.

The stalemate continued for a few days.

My mother confided in me that my father had started liking my work style. This came as a surprise to me, as I had always assumed that he didn't pay much attention to such matters.

My mother informed me that he had been observing my approach and was particularly impressed by my ability to give people space to work independently.

One of the things my father admired about my work style was my keen eye for detecting when someone was slacking off. I had developed a knack for recognizing when someone was not putting in their best effort and would intervene only when necessary. This approach not only ensured that the work was being done efficiently, but it also allowed individuals to feel trusted and empowered in their roles.

Another aspect of my work style that my father appreciated was the way I treated everyone equally and respectfully. I firmly believed in creating a positive and inclusive work environment, where everyone felt valued and heard. This not only boosted morale among the workers but also fostered a sense of unity and camaraderie within the team.

What impressed my father the most was my light-hearted comments to encourage the workers to work more efficiently

On the contrary, my brother had a serious demeanor despite being a workaholic. He always carried a sense of tension, constantly striving to prove his worth. Unfortunately, his marriage was far from happy. My sister-in-law, coming from a broken home background, had ambitious aspirations. She relentlessly nagged my brother, always wanting the best for herself.

Furthermore, she insisted on involving her good-for-nothing brother in our family business, despite my father's clear refusal. This only added to her nagging. As a result, my brother's unhappiness manifested in his behavior, leading to constant conflicts with the workers. Due to these circumstances, my father relied on me to take on more responsibilities.

After enduring countless days of family drama, we finally reached a compromise. I made a promise to pursue my paramilitary career and swimming for a maximum of five years. Following my training and a few more years of service, I would then resign and return to the family business.

However, reaching this decision was not an easy task. Both my father and I held firmly onto our positions. It was my mother who ultimately mediated the agreement, suggesting a middle path. As a result, the target date for me to take over the family business was set for early 2015.

Little did we know fate had other plans in store for us.

CHAPTER

Beginning the cause

Yang completed her graduation in the year 2012. Sources at TRM hinted that the Chinese had lost interest in the SWIFT hack case, but still looking for the girl who accompanied Ming.

She started slowly again, initially with promoting the Tibetan cause in India, Nepal, with some trips to various European countries. She continued doing that for the next five years. Her track record was good, and her planning, exemplary.

In 2017, she was to be elevated to the next level. Her seniors at TRM suggested she should move to London to embark on the next journey.

In India, there was a new government in 2014. The new Prime minister had promised to help for the Tibetan cause. And as per the grapevine, the plan mutually benefitted both India and Tibet.

In one of the meetings with the Indian prime minister, the spiritual leader talked about *Project Wall* initiated by G9 and CIA. He expressed his unhappiness with the project as it was based on violence. He wanted a peaceful solution.

Moreover, it was a known fact that once Tibet was free, it would encounter economic obstacles. The Indian prime minister had already come up with strategies to tackle this issue and had discussed them with G9. Now, he also revealed these plans to his holiness.

Well, Tibetans were thankful to India for providing shelter for the refugees. But there was no better help than helping them return home. The new prime minster in India, had promised Tibetans that hope. Yang was aware about this and was ready to be a part of this history in making.

Before this, she shared the desire for the blessings from the spiritual leader, His Holiness before her embarkation on this new life.

It was a fine sunny morning in July of 2017. Yang was to travel to Dharamsala to meet his Holiness.

This was perhaps the third or fourth time, she was getting a chance to see his Holiness, but this was their first one-o-one.

The meeting with His Holiness was brief. His Holiness was already briefed about Yang's achievements, and Holiness, in his calm, soft voice, spoke to her directly:

His Holiness: Jullay. Khamzang inalay (Hello. How are you?)

Yang: Chatsle jullay (respectful Hello). Khamzang lay, took jay shay (I am fine, thank you.)

His Holiness: Gnya Hago, Neerang ma gerragan ghella dook Tibet ley (I understand you have worked very well and wish to continue to work for Tibet.)

Yang: Kasa, Took jay shay. (Yes, thank you.)

His Holiness: Kho ma ghella dook. Shangchoos, ma nyanpo tsor rra. (You are a good girl. You need to be a bit careful, but I'll like it if you help the cause.)

His Holiness did not appreciate any sort of violence. He was not very happy with Yang's earlier episode with Ming. He again made it clear that whatever Yang does, it should not involve any sort of violence.

Thereafter His Holiness raised his hand to bless Yang. This was a sign; the meeting was over.

One of his assistants, accompanied Yang to the main monastery, where she was to be further instructed. There were further vows, prayers, and instructions in the monastery, and after two hours, the documentation and funding for her further 'education' was arranged. The ask was only one. Work for the cause of Tibet and without violence.

After the meeting a thought disturbed Yang the most. How the hell they can further the cause without being tolerable to violence.

Only time will tell.

His Holiness had banned all sorts of weapons in the monasteries. But the monks were trained for the unarmed combat, should there be any need to defend oneself.

In Yang's case, she was going for a special mission. She was now the responsibility of His Holiness and was a representative of Tibet. While she was instructed not to initiate any sort of violence, should she be subjected to any, she should defend herself good.

Now, as the cause was big and much was at stake, Yang was to be sent for a six-month advance training in London.

Without her knowledge, a dossier containing all the work done by her was already shared with the lead agent in New Delhi, who was called 'The Prince'. It was considered that; Prince was tasked by the National Security Advisor of India to recruit a special team to secure Indian borders. Liberation of Tibet was also a part of the wider plan.

The part which was not shared with anyone was The Prince had no official records and his team also had to be kept that way.

In London, there was a select group of individuals, who embarked on a journey that would forever change their lives. These individuals were the chosen recruits of Prince's army, an intelligence agency created by Prince himself.

The year was 2017. What Prince briefed his new army, was, that the new Indian government wanted nothing else, but a developed, stronger, and wealthy nation, which could withstand any and every resistance, be it political, military, or financial.

This is when, as per Prince, the idea of an independent Tibet took shape. If Tibet regains its stature of a buffer state between India and China, there would be a completely secure Northern Indian border. India had promised His Holiness, a stronger Tibet, with His Holiness reoccupying the supreme leader's position in Tibet. This would allow India most relief, as then China would not be breathing on India's neck, any further.

As Yang and the chosen ones entered the hallowed halls of the training academy in London, they were greeted by a team of seasoned instructors who would mould them into skilled Intelligence Agents. The academy was run by a retired London Police Captain called Jon Russel.

The first phase of training focused on physical fitness and endurance. Early mornings were filled with intense workouts, from strength training to rigorous cardio sessions. Yang pushed herself beyond her limits, determined to excel in every aspect of the training program.

She was already a master of disguise. To further enhance her such abilities, Yang and other trainees were provided professional training for the same.

They learned how to assume false identities, change their appearance, and convincingly portray different characters. Makeup artists and costume designers worked closely, transforming the trainees into someone unrecognizable.

Yang found herself relishing the challenge of slipping into new roles and blending seamlessly into different environments.

Next came the mental and intellectual challenges. Yang found herself immersed in an immersive classroom environment, learning the intricacies of intelligence analysis, cryptography, and counterintelligence.

She honed her analytical skills, studying patterns, deciphering codes, and developing a keen eye for detail.

The instructors pushed her to think critically, teaching her to assess situations from multiple angles and anticipate the actions of adversaries.

As her training progressed, Yang moved into the realm of operational tradecraft. She learned the art of surveillance, studying techniques used to tail targets discreetly, blend into crowds, and gather vital intelligence without arousing suspicion. Yang spent countless hours practicing these skills, perfecting the art of observation, and shadowing her assigned subjects.

Field exercises provided Yang with real-world simulations that tested her newly acquired skills. Under the watchful eye of experienced agents, she engaged in complex scenarios, where split-second decisions could mean the difference between success and failure, life and death. The exercises pushed her to the brink, simulating high-stress situations and forcing her to think on her feet.

Yang's instructors also emphasized the importance of emotional intelligence and human psychology. She learned how to read people, detect their vulnerabilities, and exploit them for strategic advantage. Understanding the motivations, fears, and desires of individuals became a crucial tool in her arsenal. She trained in negotiation and persuasion, learning how to extract information while maintaining trust and rapport.

The final phase of her training focused on teamwork and collaboration. Yang was assigned to a group of fellow trainees, each with their own unique skill sets.

They underwent intensive exercises that fostered cohesion, trust, and effective communication. Together, they honed their ability to work seamlessly as a unit, relying on each other's strengths to overcome obstacles.

As the day of graduation approached, Yang and her fellow trainees stood on the precipice of their new lives as Agency's operatives. They had transformed from ordinary individuals into highly skilled intelligence agents, ready to embark on dangerous missions in service of their country. Their training had prepared them for the challenges that lay ahead, but they knew that the real test would be on the field.

In a solemn ceremony, Yang and her comrades received their official agency credentials. They took an oath to uphold the values of integrity, courage, and loyalty that defined their profession. The weight of their responsibility settled upon their shoulders as they prepared to venture into the shadows, protecting their nation from threats both seen and unseen.

As Yang walked out of the training facility, she carried with her the lessons, skills, and indomitable spirit that would guide her in the world of espionage. The path ahead would be treacherous and unpredictable, but she was prepared. With unwavering resolve and an unbreakable bond with her fellow agents, Yang stepped into the unknown, ready to serve as the shield and sword of the agency, defending her country and preserving peace.

Before she moved out of the academy, she was called by Jon Russel in his office. Here, she found Prince already seated. She was told to move to Brick Lane, London, where an apartment was already booked for her. She was asked to enrol in a course in Kings College. She was to come in contact with certain *Students*, who are chosen for her. Prince gave her an address in Central London, where she will stay with a small group of *Students*.

This was her first assignment for Project *Brihadratha*.

CHAPTER 08

The Cop

March 2011, I started my training at the training academy in Hyderabad. It was 48 weeks of training. We were some 150 odd officers, who joined the academy.

The initial few days were tough for most amongst us. Barring me and a few other officers who had been athletes, most of the cadets complained about body pain from continuous running and exercising. Most of them were studious ones. Competed well educationally but were less exposed to outdoors.

So, during the initial few days, we had some seven AWOLs. After confirming their safe return home, academy authorities removed their names as cadets.

We gradually started our training with running, physical exercise, rope climbing, pullups, pushups, and marching lessons. The day was divided into four sessions, early morning physical training, which included PT and Parade. Post breakfast, three hours of indoor classes on law and governance. One hour break for lunch and some rest then another two hours of parade and weaponry training. Later, the evening was for outdoor sports.

Came the first Saturday, while we expected a lighter training schedule, the day started with a ten-kilometer road run, alternating to walk after every few kilometers.

This became a routine, every alternate Saturday.

On one such road run, we were passing through a small cluster of houses near Mir Alam Tank. The dwellers came out of their houses hearing our boot steps. Soon, we encountered a heard of sheep on the way.

We kept on running, another few hundred meters, to realize that there was a lamb running along with us, within the formation. While the girls within the formation advised others to be cautious and not to step on the poor chap, Hemant Barua, the Assamese guy who was the most notorious amongst us, shushed everyone.

By the evening, the owner of the lamb came to our academy, looking for the lamb. Lakhbir, a Sikh within us confidants, was on sentry duty. The Hyderabadi lamb owner could not understand Punjabi, so Lakhbir alerted us, in Gurbani style:

Jinha di si memani – (the owner of the lamb)

Aa pahunche darbaar, - (is in the house)

Dhakkan shakkan kas lao, - (tighten the lid on the cooking pot)

Bhap na aaye bahar. - (so, the aroma doesn't come out)

It was then, our trainers came to know, that the poor chap was already in the cooking pot.

It was a Saturday, a day when we could have our fill on liquor and good food. What better way than to enjoy your own kill?

But that had to wait. It was not until we completed four rounds of the ground, holding the rifle high in our hands, that we could enjoy this special meal. The girls and other cadets wondered why there was a special punishment for the seven of us.

While the punishment was an enjoyment for us, the sad part was, the lamb had to be shared with the four trainers as well, who were our new confidantes.

Gradually the distance of our road run and walk was to increase to 35 kilometers during the 30th week. By the 38th weekend, we were to have the road run exam, wherein we were given an additional weight of 50 kilograms, in the form of sacks, rifle and holdall bag. To qualify, we were to complete these 30 kilometers run within three hours.

The average running speed for good runners is 15 KMPH. We all were good runners, but an additional hour was given, as this was road run and walk with an additional 50 KGs wight on our bodies.

For girls, an additional half hour was provided.

By mid-year our bodies had become so tough that any form of physical excursion did not bother us at all. We often used to find ways to humor ourselves with physical punishments. One cadet purposely would make a mistake, resulting in the whole platoon facing consequences such as extra runs, pushups, crunches, or frog jumps. Surprisingly, this was not only amusing for the other platoons but also for the cadet's own group.

The academy had a strong emphasis on discipline. The residential buildings for men & women were separate, located in opposite directions. The training grounds and administrative building were situated in between them. There was a significant distance of one kilometer between the two buildings, and it was strictly forbidden for students of one gender to enter the premises of the other, no matter the circumstances.

Our training prepared us for exciting adventures. As a result, a select few adventurers put their training to the test. Utilizing the cover of darkness, they would stealthily navigate their way to the desired location, entering and exiting through windows without a sound. Whatever free time they had on hand, they would spend with their chosen ones.

The majority of trainees were exhausted and slept soundly. It was only in the morning; the tired eyes and a special smile would make the fellow cadets realize that the couple had enjoyed each other's company.

Nevertheless, due to the demanding daily schedule, the non-adventurous cadets could only look on with envy.

In July, a specially recruited Batch from Nagaland arrived for training.

We had always heard that dog meat was considered a delicacy in Nagaland, but it wasn't until we noticed a decrease in the number of dogs within the academy that we realized it was true. The Nagas had their own methods of obtaining dog blood and meat, using any sharp object, their hands and hunting techniques.

Dogs are never allowed in training camps or academies. Prior to the Nagas joining, Trilochan Singh, the Havildar in charge of our armory, was allotted .22 bullets every few months to deal with the dogs. On Sundays, when most of the cadets were out in the city, the remaining ones were advised to stay indoors to prevent any accidental stray bullets.

However, with the arrival of the Naga Batch, those bullets were no longer needed.

During our training, we learnt rock climbing, horse riding, unarmed combat, using various weapons, knives and also silencing our enemies with bare hands. Creating different strategies during any calamity or crises was also taught during indoor training.

My best week was the week when the cadets were taught swimming, as for qualifying the final exam, one had to swim at least 100 meters. While most others struggled during the week, I volunteered and coached a few. Felt like a hero during the entire week.

It was during this week; I came really close to Sarika Arora. She gave some good vibes; hence we became a couple soon.

After swimming week, during most mornings, I had puffy eyes, as sleep was replaced with adventure.

Time went fast as we did not have much time for ourselves. Soon it was February 2012, the last month of our training. The entire month we practiced for our passing out parade.

I had excelled in training and was adjudged the best cadet. This could be due to the excellent physical fitness because of swimming and perhaps my disciplined life, even before joining the Forces.

As the best cadet, I commanded our passing out parade. My whole family was specially invited to this event. My father, still sullen, but I could see pride in his eyes, when I started commanding the parade. I could also see dampness in his eyes, while he placed pips on my shoulders.

That was my father. Never acknowledging his love or pride but secretly felt proud whatever I did.

My mom told me, back home, he was shouting with joy when they received the special invitation. Dad went on bragging to everyone he met that his son was the best cadet.

But here, he kept his emotions under control.

It was only after the pipping ceremony that my father hugged me. It was a tight hug, which told me he was sobbing. He did not leave me, till he was normal again.

I had never seen him emotional. This was new for me.

Sarika came to meet my parents. She had to join the Karnataka cadre, while my cadre was Jammu and Kashmir. While my mother judged love in her eyes for me, it was totally indifference from my end.

I know, I am bad in this respect, but can't help. That is how I am built. Can never remain attached to anything or anyone.

After the passing out parade, we were allowed a ten-day holiday, during which we could go to our homes.

That's what I did, accompanied my family back home.

During those ten days, it was almost a daily routine that I would go to Talkatora swimming pool. I was treated as a celebrity here.

Every day, I saw Ms. Dolma and at least for once, I was reminded of Yang, while seeing her.

Yes, I never could get attached to anyone, but Yang did not leave my thoughts. I never asked and Ms. Dolma never told, where Yang was. There was no discussion around her.

Ten days were over soon, it was time to join my active duty.

My first posting was in Ladakh, the Northern region of Jammu and Kashmir. I joined here in April first week of 2012. The region was low on oxygen levels. One had to get acclimatized to this low oxygen, which took some days. I was just over 22 years old at that time, was physically fit, possessed powerful lungs due to swimming, hence there was not much trouble for me to adapt to this high-altitude region.

Ladakh is a border region. This part of the Indian border is strategic for the country, as on one side, it is Pakistan occupied Kashmir, which is a constant threat to India. But the major portion of the border was under threat by China, post it occupied Tibet.

Till year 1950, the Indian borders with China were secured due to the independent country of Tibet. Tibet worked as a buffer between India and China. However, in 1950, when China invaded Tibet, this buffer faded.

The Tibetan government led by the spiritual leader continued to rule Tibet till 1959. When the threat to his life from Chinese government increased, he was persuaded by his followers to leave Tibet.

The Leader escaped to India through Ladakh. He wanted to settle in Ladakh, as the topography was similar with Tibet, but the Indian government, considering continuous threat to his life, persuaded him to move to Dharamsala, in Himachal Pradesh.

Now, as there was no independent state of Tibet, the Indian border was open and easily accessible to China.

There had been numerous attempts by China to invade India. Considerable portion of land was encroached by China during the year 1962 war. Hence the region of Ladakh remained of military importance.

It is funny. Tibet is encroached by China. While Europe discussed about Kashmir being illegally occupied by India, they conveniently forgot to discuss about Pakistan occupied Kashmir or China occupied Tibet and Ladakh. Or for that matter Britain occupied Scotland / Ireland. It is power which changes perception. Britain and China being powerful, the political leaders dare not speak against them.

Ladakh is a beautiful place. The region itself is bounded by two of the world's mightiest mountain ranges, the Great Himalaya, and the Karakoram. Ladakh is mystical in all the spheres it covers, from nature, geography, sceneries to the modest cultures that it fosters.

It is said that only in Ladakh a person sitting in the sun with his feet in the shade can suffer from sunstroke and frostbite at the same time. The temperature could be hot, even in midst of snow, as this is a high-altitude desert.

As for Ladakhi people, their features suggest their different built. Like the land itself, the people of Ladakh are usually quite different from those in the rest of India. The faces and physique of the Ladakhis, and the clothes they wear, are more similar to those of Tibet and Central Asia, than of India.

Their foreheads are broad, which is believed to be developed by nature to conserve more oxygen for brain. It is, perhaps for this reason, while a person from the other part of the world feels restless traveling in Ladakh, Ladakhis feel no such issues.

Initially, for me, language was an issue here. Language spoken in Ladakh is Bhoti and Purgi, which are Sino-Tibetan languages, with no similarities with Hindi, which I spoke.

As my cadre was Jammu and Kashmir, I was taught Dogri and Kashmiri in basic training. But Bhoti and Purgi, I had to learn here. Most of the people under my command were from Ladakh. They had picked up Hindi due to their experience in serving in the force. So, they were my interpreters, while we communicated with any local Ladakhi. Being a quick learner, in the next two months, I was fluent, even with the accent.

Ladakh being close to Tibet, there were many Tibetans settled there. They never had any difficulties with the language or topography.

Chatting with the Tibetans, I realized their sorry state of affairs. While they had received official resident permissions from Indian government, they missed their homes, back in Tibet.

For them, their spiritual leader is God. It pained them, that he was dethroned in their own home country, and he and his followers were forced to live in exile.

Tibetans also shared horror stories about Chinese, who targeted Tibetans back home. The local Tibetans were treated as second rate citizens. As they sided with his Holiness, they were also treated as traitors.

I came in contact with Tashi Deleh, who was a Tibetan story writer and teller, in his mid-fifties. Tashi told me, that he came to India as a toddler. His father had initially stayed in Dharamsala. Later, Tashi went to Bangalore University for higher studies. After completing his studies, he came back to Dharamshala and now to Ladakh to serve the Tibetan community.

He had made it his point, to tell the stories about Tibet and Tibetans, to preserve their oral history. He travelled across the country and also to international destinations, where he shared the stories of Tibet and gathered support for the Tibetan cause. This he had been doing for the past 30 odd years.

Tashi further told me that he started this project by listening to a friend, who was currently in Australia. He was a former political prisoner. Listening to his stories, Tashi found them moving, inspiring and encouraging. He asked him why he did not share them with others. The friend told Tashi, that this was common knowledge within the Tibetan community. But Tashi thought that this should not only remain within, but should be shared internationally, through the internet or social media. Hence, he started writing origin stories about different Tibetan individuals and spreading the same through internet and through books.

Tashi also helped Tibetans, to learn to communicate in global languages, so the stories of Tibet could be told, wherever they went. Tashi wanted them to have basic communication skills and also basic knowledge, like how to send an email, how to use social media and all those kinds of things.

Tashi would tell me horror stories, which Tibetans faced during China's aggression. Most of this knowledge was told to him by his elders, as he was very young, when he migrated to India with his father. His mother was killed.

He told me that his mother was the second cousin of his holiness, the spiritual leader or Lama, as he was called.

When the lama left Tibet, his followers and family was tortured by the Chinese. Tashi's maternal uncle, his wife and Tashi's mother were taken into custody. They were given massive pain to provide information about his holiness. When they provided none, first their knees were broken, their nails were plucked, skin was burnt with cigarettes and were left to die.

Many others were left in the same painful state. The women were raped repeatedly, left nude for other soldiers to rape, as and when they wanted. And finally, when they died, their bodies were hung on poles, outside their homes for others to see, still unclothed. The bodies remained like that for a few months, and were only cremated, when the Chinese left for their cities.

While I was still learning more about the Tibetans, I was nominated for the much-dreaded Commando course for the Indian Forces. This four-month course was so tough that the passing rate was just over 40%.

While 20% of the trainees opted out during the first few weeks due to strenuous routine, more than 40% could not clear the tough examination or suffered injuries during the training.

I, being the all-round best cadet during basic training, was the natural selection for this course. So, from September 2012, I was shifted to Mussoorie, a hills station in India, where the commando training is provided.

CHAPTER

Commando

The course was much more than the horror stories we had heard about it. First few weeks, the dropout rate was more than the official percentage.

In all, we were 78 trainees nominated for the course, of which 72 reported. The training academy was on a hill, and naturally, the passages were not planes. The first day started at 05:00. The sun had not yet risen, but we were supposed to be lined up at the training grounds, post our daily routines, fully dressed.

Being fresh out of basic training, getting up and getting ready was not an issue. The temperature, however, was.

The temperature outside being around 12☐ C, we had to cover ourselves well, in slacks and sweatshirt, all whites. By the evening, these whites were just a shade less brown, due to the extreme workouts on the ground. Due to extreme workout, within first 30 minutes, the sweatshirts were off, which remained clean. We worked out in vests.

The challenge was, again, the next day, as our clothes had to be white. So, we were given six sets of clothing, each for every day of the week, while the next week, they had to be ready for a repeat.

The clothing was the least of challenges. The main challenge was the strenuous workouts every day. The first day workout started, with a kilometer walk, squatting down.

You may try that for 10 meters, you'll know, about what I am talking. For this, one needs to sit in squatting position and move forward. Next day, one comes to know about the effect. It is impossible to sit on the commode or even to sit otherwise.

While this was the beginning, the work out included frog jumps, pushups, pull ups, sprints, horse jumps, rope climbing, mountain and wall climbing, rappelling, trench jumps, zigzags, 14 feet jumps, the list is endless. All this was part of the 4+4 hours, daily routine.

During the evening, we had the additional time for two hours 'for leisure', during which we had to play some game. The challenge was, that the game one could choose was only from Tennis, Basketball, Volleyball, squash, or football. No wonder, before the end of the second week, we were left only 48, with a steep 33% opting out.

Next came the injuries.

During the first week, I had bonded well with Gurinder and Manmohan, both my fellow cadets from basic training. During the third day of our training, we embarked on our first jump from a specially designed 14 feet platform. This jump serves as a crucial preparation for commandos, enabling them to effectively pursue and apprehend criminals in case of an escape. The technique for the jump is to roll the moment you touch the ground, so the body weight does not hit the shins.

Gurinder seemed to have forgotten the technique and was subjected to a hairline fracture on his shin bone after a jump. Despite the pain, he chose not to see a doctor and kept training with the injury. It must have been excruciating for him to run with a fractured shin.

Eventually, during another jump on the eighth day, his shin gave out, causing the bone to tear through the flesh. He was immediately taken to the hospital and then sent back home with a leg cast.

It took four years for Gurinder to walk without a limp.

Now, it was Manmohan who was my confidant during the training, along with a steadily decreasing number, who left due to various such injuries.

By the last week, we were finally left 36, just 50%, who succeeded in clearing the final exam. I was lucky to be amongst the clearing number. Here, just passing the exam counted. There were no marks for being a hero or top the exams.

I was back in Ladakh during February 2013. I was leaner, had added more muscles and was extremely confident, which showed in my walk. I missed swimming, as it was out of the question in this region. We had our officers' clubhouse, which offered many sports, but swimming.

During most part of the year, the water in the pipelines and water tanks froze. We had to keep our taps partially running during the nights, so we could get water for our morning routines.

We had many lakes in Ladakh, but swimming in the same was not advised, the water was freezing cold and, the lakes were in the direct view of the Chinese soldiers, who had the advantage of height.

So, in my free time, I started learning more about Ladakh and Tibet. This continued for the next another year or so. More I learnt, more I got attached to the culture and more I hated the Chinese for bringing such torture and suffering to the Tibetans. This region was full of such stories about tortures.

By now, I was convinced that had Tibet been an independent country, India would not have to spend much on the military, guarding the borders 24/7.

Around 85% of Sino-India border, could have been separated from China, as this large area of land belonged to Tibet. Tibetans, being God fearing, calm and much unlike the cunning Chinese, would have been much better neighbors for India.

I used to have these detailed discussions with Tashi and other Tibetan exiles, and these discussions confirmed my believe about independent Tibet.

Once over a few drinks, I discussed these thoughts with my Commander. He did not reply, but stated, "You are different. You should join the agency".

Being young and comparatively inexperienced, I never thought that these talks were being recorded in my confidential personal file and one day would decide my future career.

It was a fine Friday evening in Delhi in December 2015. My parents were happy, as I was returning home for a short stay.

As promised to my father, I was to resign soon. This short visit to Delhi was in respect of knowing about the relieving formalities.

This trip involved official work. I had taken an additional two holidays, to spend with my parents. On Sunday, I was to fly back to Jammu and then Ladakh.

At the headquarters, I was told by an officer that Ramkumar, an officer from the intelligence bureau, wants to meet me.

I saw no reason why he should meet me, but the officer persisted. The meeting was supposed to be short, but it took around two hours to complete.

The officer took me to an empty meeting room and asked if I would be interested in working for the bureau.

I declined the offer, as I was about to leave the Force. The officer persisted and said that I would be an asset to the bureau.

I thanked him for the complement but stated that this is not what my family wants.

"What about you?", he asked.

I took a pause, thought, then replied,

"It does not matter, as I am leaving the force soon."

I would not know if he could sense sadness in my voice.

I started to get up, and as for me, the meeting was over.

Ramkumar continued, as I got up -

"Well actually, this is more of facilitator kind of role, what we have in mind for you".

Seeing interest in my eyes, he continued,

"You see, the world is changing. It's no longer, that everything can be achieved with violence. In the changed world, countries need negotiators and influencers. We see that in you".

I knew it did not matter to me, still out of curiosity, I asked what he had in mind.

Ramkumar continued,

"The government of India has a plan to rule the hearts of the world. The new Prime Minister wants, that India should be the supreme economy and should be the world influencer".

"By now, you would be aware of the kind of support the new prime minister has received from the world leaders. You would also have seen the kind of investments; India has received in last one year. The world is looking at India as a new investment destination".

"We have elaborate plans, to utilize our trained and educated large population and become the manufacturing hub for the world. Our talent should gain all the employment in India itself, to further curtail the brain drain".

I argued, "do you think it is possible with the kind of security scenarios we have in India? Half of our revenue is lost in securing our borders and salvaging the loss created by terrorist acts. Moreover, the terrorist attacks hinder the 'safe investment destination' tag for India. To my mind, we need to first plan eradicating these hindrances, before we want to achieve the desired goal".

Ramkumar took a small pause, then continued.

"You see, these thoughts you have, have drawn us towards you. You actually know about the problem, so it has not to be explained to you. Don't you think, people with the same wavelength, having the same thoughts, who understand the issues, would be asset for this new India"?

He continued, "we are also aware about your thoughts on liberation of Tibet and how it can help India save millions, being spent now on safeguarding the borders. We have the same thoughts as you, that the liberation would make India safe. We also know that you can help us achieve that. Won't you want to be a part of that history in making?"

Now, it was my turn to take a pause. I remembered my commander encouraging me towards the agency, stating that I would be an asset to the agency.

When once, I had said that 'I wanted to, but was bound by family commitments', he had said, that the family should not come in between your and country's decision.

I told Ramkumar that it was not for me to decide now. I had to ask my father again.

Perhaps, that was a wrong answer.

I knew my father's answer, but the proposition excited me. So, I wanted to try it out.

Before I left the room, Ramkumar said "while I appreciate your love and respect for your parents, it would be good, if you decide in favor, before you go back to your unit".

Seeing my agitated expressions, as I had sensed a threat, the way it was spoken, he smiled and said, "pardon my south Indian accent, it came out differently. But we all would love to work with you. We would be happy if you are able to change your parents' mind".

That day, I reached home around 08:30 PM. My father was waiting for me with a drink in his hand. I could see him getting emotional seeing me. We were actually meeting after a gap of over three years. I had not come home during these three years.

In these years, as I knew that I was aiming to leave the force in a short while, I was taking this opportunity to learn as much as I could. I had completed an advanced mountaineering course, an advanced survival course, which trained a person to survive in extreme cold, at high altitude, under water, and even without food and water for a longer duration. The last three years had been really grilling. I already had a lean body due to swimming, but now I looked really tough.

This was the first time my dad offered me a drink. I hesitated, as our family values did not permit us to drink before elders.

My father winked, and said, "You are old enough now. We can enjoy a drink together".

To his surprise, I did not stop before three. At about 10:00 PM, my brother came back from the factory. We all had dinner together, which was personally prepared by my mother.

Next two days, I spent every minute with my parents and brother, who remained home to spend time with me.

I brought up the conversation I had with Ramkumar. My parents were elated, and I could see the pride in their eyes.

Of course, it was a matter of pride for a business family, their son was being considered for an important assignment for the country. Also, it was good for them to know that I cared for their decision.

But the answer was the same. I had to return to business.

Next two days, both my parents kept telling me, how I should refuse. My father sharing his experience continued, "you know, your answer should be polite. Politely refuse, that due to the family responsibilities, you cannot join. They should not feel indignant. I know, the government could be bad and can destroy the business, if you rub them on the wrong side. Put that on us, that we don't want you to continue".

I felt like I was being briefed on how to deal with an outraged teacher during my school days. Having grown up in last four years in the law enforcement, I knew, what the repercussions could be, if I put the blame on my parents.

I kept mum, but before leaving for Jammu, I called Ramkumar and shared the decision. It was my decision. I was looking forward to an easy, protected life.

"So, it's a NO".

I didn't know then, or even after five years, that by then, the damage was already done.

I went back to Jammu, and then onwards to Leh. During my stay in Leh, there were at least six meetings with various officers whom I did not know, who kept insisting that I reconsider my decision about leaving the force. I was fit and they had the right opportunity for me.

As I had made up my mind, or rather my father had made up a mind for me, I kept insisting that I would leave.

My commander, during one such meeting, advised me to reconsider, for the sake of my family. I didn't know he was serious.

I said jokingly, I am leaving for my family.

It was just past midnight on February 14-15, 2016, I woke up drenched in sweat. I had a bad dream. I could see my mother trying to say something but was not able to communicate. Her face was covered in something red, and I could see my father lying by her side, not moving at all.

It was some strange place, suddenly a group of people came shouting near my parents. The scene changed to be of a road, with vehicles honking. The group tried to forcefully pick up both my parents. I was also a part of that group and was trying to protect my parents. This is when I woke up.

Next morning, Suresh, my commander, called me to his office. I was expecting the usual pleasant face, but saw a somber one, as if someone had died.

In a deep somber voice, Suresh informed me that my parents had met with an accident last night. They were critical. Suresh had already arranged for my flight back home. I had to leave immediately.

That's for my last night dream...

It was the morning of February 16, 2016. I was still in shock.

In the last four+ years of service with the armed forces, I saw many casualties. I had seen the men, with whom I had dined a few minutes ago, torn to pieces, when they stepped over live landmines. My colleagues, with whom I had shared many hours of laughter, being dead, as an enemy bullet found them as a target. I had carried bodies of my friends, cried silently on their bodies, at the same time keeping a strong face, so my men are not demoralized. I had learnt to control my emotions the hardest way.

But today was totally different. I was to see the dead bodies of my most beloved people. People, who had brought me to this world. People, who were my true well-wishers, who would never think anything which did not favor me. They were lying in front of me, motionless and emotionless.

I loved my father so much that for his wish, was looking forward to joining his business. It was just to ease out his world.

It was just a few days more, I would have been discharged from service, to join my family permanently.

Perhaps, this was not what fate wanted for me.

I had landed in Delhi from Leh early morning. My journey was arranged by my commander through an army helicopter. There had been inconsistent snowfall at Leh airport for the past several days and all commercial flights were cancelled. I was supposed to fly yesterday by the same helicopter; however, it could not be done, due to bad weather.

On reaching home, I hugged my brother. He was still not accepting the fact that we both were orphaned. My sister-in-law was also shocked. No one expected this tragedy.

The bodies of my parents had still not been released by the police. Being an accidental death, legal formalities had to be completed. My brother informed me that the police conducted a postmortem last evening. Since they did not see any foul play, promised to release the bodies today morning.

I was curious to know, my father, who was an alert driver and never drove under the influence of alcohol, how he could meet with such an accident.

My brother, being under shock, had no answer to this, in fact, he had not questioned this to anyone, including the cops.

He came to know about the tragedy at about midnight of 14-15. Our parents had gone for a party to friends' house, who were celebrating their 25th wedding anniversary. At about 12:30, he received a call from our father's phone.

The car was giving some trouble, so he thought, that father would be calling to say, perhaps he is stuck someplace and would be requesting him to pick them up. But he was surprised to hear an unidentified person, talking in frantic voice, claiming that the owner of the phone had met with an accident.

At first, he thought that this could be a prank or some kind of fraud call, as many such instances had happened in Delhi, especially during winter nights. People were called to secluded places by claiming to be relatives, and then were robbed.

To double check, my brother called our mother's phone. That one also was picked up by the same person, who stated that he is a constable from Delhi Police. He is taking our parents to Max hospital in Saket. This is when the realization hit my brother.

He knew that our parents had gone to the farmhouse of their friends at Chhattarpur. As we stayed in New Friends colony, the route matched. Also, the person answering the phone had both the phones in his possession and he was calling him to the hospital.

He left immediately, in his pajamas. Being nighttime, he could reach Max in just 10 minutes. But those 10 minutes were the worst of his life. On reaching the hospital, he came across just the bodies, with no life.

Having grown up in a protective environment, my brother had not seen any tragedies. And this was, the greatest of all, for him to handle. He lost his conscience for some time, until the doctors treated him and brought him back.

There was a police constable, who had taken my parents to the hospital. He informed that this is a medico-legal case, and they would require to conduct a postmortem.

Still under shock, my brother was given a sedative, and the same constable dropped him home.

It was my sister-in-law, who took charge, thereon, and started informing our relatives, friends, and of course, called my commander. Being posted at high-altitude, we never had access to direct phones, hence, she could not call me.

At about 10:00 AM on February 16th, we both, along with my uncle, left for Safdarjung hospital, where the postmortem was conducted last evening. And at about 12:30, we could get the bodies. The officer-in-charge, being told about my background, directed me to a stationed police officer, as I wanted to know, what happened.

The police officer, saluted me and then shared the details, as noted in the police records.

Last night was quite foggy and as the drive was through the green zone on Chhatterpur – Mehroli road, the visibility was really low. My father was at the wheel, driving within permissible speed.

As he turned right from Laddha Sarai, he did not stop at the red signal. An army truck, coming from Sultanpur side, did not see his grey color car, followed the green signal and thus, hit the car in full speed.

The officer shared that both my parents lost their life within seconds and were brought dead, at the hospital.

This looked strange to me. I had never seen my father jumping a signal. In fact, when I and my brother were learning to drive, he was very strict on observing traffic discipline.

The postmortem report supported the above theory; hence the bodies were released to us.

This was really emotional now. People, who had always hugged us, at any given opportunity, were lying motionless. I remember my mother's words. As I was growing up, I used to shrug her efforts to hug me, as I found the gesture childish.

My mother used to say, "You are lucky that you have adoring parents, and you are able to get these hugs. One day, you will miss all this, and will remember these words".

Yes, mom, I really miss that hug, now.

I and my brother hugged them and could not control our tears. We cried uncontrollably for some 15 minutes, until my uncle raised us up and consoled us.

All the deaths, I had seen and all the people I had killed, this was the time, when I understood the value of life. How, I would give anything, if just once, my mother could call my name, or my father could smile at me.

We took our parents home in an ambulance.

Our living room was full of relatives and friends, however unlike on most occasions, the mood was gloomy.

This room had seen many celebrations, as my parents were considered to be great hosts. The relatives and friends, who had enjoyed such hospitality, were here once again, to pay their last respects, to this lovely couple.

My mother was always brimming with life when there was a party in the house. She was always beside my father. She still was, however, today she was lying on floor, covered with a white sheet, still very close to her life partner.

Soon, Panditji performed last rites pooja, after which, we took them both to the crematorium.

The crematorium was overflowing with our relatives and friends. My father had been a popular man and so was my mother. Apart from being a successful businessman, my father had been an ace sportsman.

While growing up in our Friends Colony house, there were hardly any weekend we had seen, there were no visits from any of our relatives or their friends. He still had a large fan following from the sports enthusiasts. Also, as he sponsored budding sports persons, he had a large following before them as well.

My mother had been managing her own pre-primary school. She had been a loving mom and the same emotion she carried with her young students as well. The parents of these students were shocked to hear about the news of her demise. Most of them made it a point to attend the funeral.

Just before sunset, the funeral piers were lit by my brother, being the elder son. He was crying uncontrollably. I tried my level best to stay calm, but the moment piers caught fire, I kneeled, and the emotions came overflowing.

There was no stopping thereafter, for at least 15 minutes. Me and my brother kept sitting on the ash laden crematorium floor for another hour or so, till our uncle told us it was time to leave.

The relatives kept coming to us with folded hands, paying their condolences, but this was all blurry for both of us. When the last of the relatives left, it was already 07:30 PM. Only the immediate family remained in crematorium, and slowly we also left.

The ashes had to be collected the next morning, to be taken to Haridwar, later.

I had stayed back after the funeral for other Hindu rituals, and on the 14th day, I left for Leh. It took another month, and by March 20, 2016, I was back in Delhi, as a civilian.

Not having much to do socially, I reconnected with my friends. During the daytime, I started going to our factory and during evenings, it was at one friend's or the other. The routine was boring. The home and factory, continuously reminding me of my parents.

By June, I was practically frustrated with my life. I am not the one who can have a steady life or relationship. With my parents' demise, there had been quite a few disagreements with my brother and his wife.

My brother wanted the control of the factory and wanted me to work under him. I disagreed. We were on the verge of splitting the business when the call came.

The man calling from the other end introduced himself as working for The Prince.

I considered it a prank call and disconnected. The caller called again, and I did not pick up.

This continued till late evening and at about 07:30 PM, a police constable visited our house. We all thought, this visit would relate to the investigation of the accidental death of my parents, but the constable wanted to speak with me.

On meeting me, he said that there is a message from government of India, that I would have to visit the North Block (Administrative block of the Government of India), next morning. The time would be shared with me, and someone will call me regarding that.

The moment this was said I again received a call from the same unidentified number. This time I picked it up.

The person said he was speaking from Prince's office and The Prince wanted to meet me. I was to meet The Prince tomorrow morning at 11:00, not at North block, but at Vayu Sena bhavan. I should come sharp at 11:00, there would be someone to receive me at the parking lot.

This is when I realized, Prince is no other, but perhaps the code for an officer within the special bureau. I remembered the conversations I had before my release from the force.

Was the special bureau still interested in me?

Earlier it was different. I had to take over the family business and relieve my father. Even now, things were hazy, but I decided to, at least meet this, Prince.

CHAPTER 10

The Prince

Just a few days before meeting Adwait, Prince was in London. Prince owned a large estate some 70 miles from London, in Eddington.

Prince stood out from the rest of the agency staff because he did not come from a bureaucratic background. He was a true descendant of royalty, with his Royal titles being renounced even before he was born.

His mother, Gitanjali Devi, was the youngest daughter of the Maharaja of Tikhangarh, Rajasthan. During her youth, she had a passion for horse riding and excelled as a polo player. It was during this time that she became enamored with an English polo player named Edmund Wiley.

The young Princess found her heart entwined with this dashing polo player. Their love blossomed amidst the thundering hooves of the polo field, where Edmund's skill and grace caught the princess's eye.

However, their love faced insurmountable obstacles as the Maharaja disapproved of Edmund's humble background. Moreover, even if the match would have been approved by the Maharaja, the union between the princess and a British would never would have been approved by the Maharaja's courtiers.

Determined to be together, Geetanjali and Edmund decided to elope. On a moonlight night, they left the Royal Palace on their loyal horses. From Tikhangarh, they reached Jaipur and then from Jaipur, they took a train to Bombay. From Bombay, they boarded a ship to Edmund's home in Edinburg, Scotland.

The young princess eloped from the palace, leaving behind titles and responsibilities. She had hoped a comfortable life in Scotland, but on reaching Edinburg, she found Edmund to be from an ordinary peasant family. Still unperturbed, Geetanjali insisted on living with Edmund. They both settled down in a quaint village, amid lush landscapes, near Edinburg.

Within a year, the passion that was ignited on the polo field, started to weed off. The daily chores, which Geetanjali was never accustomed to performing, became the daily cause of fights between them. But when Geetanjali became pregnant, having no one to care for her during the pregnancy, she called for help.

The Maharaja, who loved his youngest the most, sent his trusted Divan to take the Princess to London, with instructions to get her child aborted and bring the princess home.

She was already in her 20th week. Although she was in great shape, the doctors refused the abortion, as due to her strenuous recent life, she had developed complications. Doctors were afraid that the abortion at this stage may end her life, or she would be bed ridden, for the rest of her life.

With abortion out of the question, the Divan consulted the Maharaja and Gitanjali devi was then married to Edmund, in a quite wedding in Edinburgh Castle Church.

As Edmund was not from a wealthy background, the Maharaja bought a large Estate in Eddington, and gifted the same to the new couple. This was early 1947.

When young Stevenson was born, India was already preparing for its Independence. As Stevenson or Steve, how he was called, being of mixed race, he could not inherit the riches of Tikhangarh Estate.

Soon, by the year 1950, the now Independent Indian government started unification of states and the title of Maharaja was taken away from Geetanjali's father.

Geetanjali had already relinquished her title as princess. However, both Edmund and Geetanjali lovingly called Stevenson, their 'Rajkumar'. The name caught up and the maids and servants at the estate, instead of calling him Rajkumar, started calling him the English translation, 'The Prince'.

The yields from Edington Estate were sufficient for a luxurious life. So, the childhood of Prince was quite safe, secure and without any care for money. Like his parents, he loved riding and by the time he was 17, he was already an established Polo player.

Prince enjoyed dual citizenship, British, as well as Indian. Due to this, travelling between these two countries was easy for him. Since his early days, having grown on an English Estate, Prince loved adventures.

Edington is near North Wessex, which is an outstandingly beautiful area. Large mountains, Valleys, waterfalls, crystal clear lakes, are in abundance in this area. While the land is different shades of green, the sky is absolutely clear blue. And in winter, when the area is under snow, it appears like a wonderland.

Eddington and Wessex were part of the Roman Empire during 4th and 5th centuries and the remains can still be seen in the city of Bath, which still has an existing Sulphur water Roman Bath.

The entire area is a treat for adventure lovers. Solo bike trips, mountaineering, cliff hanging, swimming, canoeing, sky diving, horse riding, were all part of the growing up for Prince.

Having grown in a large home, and being the only child of the Estate owners, he was privileged and always surrounded by maids and servants.

His Anglo-Indian looks, lean body and Royal mannerism, always attracted the most beautiful girls around him. He was just 15, when he lost virginity with a chambermaid, who was also the same age. From now on, sex was also included in the many adventures and pass times of Prince.

When Prince attained the age of 18, he met his maternal Grand Father for the first time. Although, his mother was not considered to be royalty anymore, but the Maharaja was old and he wished to see The Prince, before he died. The royal title was gone, still the Maharaja continued to be called one. He still owned the royal palace and a large estate.

Prince travelled to India for the first time. This was in 1965. He landed at Delhi Airport and was taken to Tikhangarh by the Royal guards. He met the Maharaja in the Royal palace. The Maharaja was highly impressed with his looks, build, and mannerism. It was tough luck; the Maharaja had no male heirs and Prince could not be accepted as a descendant.

Knowing The Prince's adventurous lifestyle, the Maharaja asked him if Prince wanted to lead his life that way.

When Prince nodded, next day Maharaja called his dear friend Ram Narayan Jain, who was heading the newly formed Indian secret service. The Maharaja introduced The Prince to Mr. Jain.

Mr. Jain liked the fact that Prince, being Indian and British Citizen, could travel without Visa to most of the Commonwealth countries. He was trained well in all sorts of un-armed combat, so he was the ideal candidate to work for the agency.

Prince never wanted any money for this work, but still, Mr. Jain ensured that his all the expenses are covered by the agency, and he would have enough at any given time, to spend on wine, or women.

The young lad, all of 18 years, trained well. He could not officially join government service due to age. He had to wait and when he was 21, he officially joined the Indian secret agency. This was in 1968.

During his 37 years long career with the agency, he was never liked by his seniors, as he never respected them, his working style was barbarian, and he seldom took his seniors' orders seriously.

Throughout his time at the agency, there were multiple instances where he faced accusations of being a double agent, also working for the CIA. However, despite numerous investigations, no concrete evidence ever emerged to substantiate these claims. Nevertheless, it was indisputable that he maintained strong connections with nearly every international secret agent, and one could rely on him to obtain information about any government from The Prince.

Due to his unruly lifestyle, Prince could never be offered the agency's top post, and he retired heading the Asian and European desk of the agency, in the year 2007.

He went back to his estate in Eddington, hoping to enjoy a carefree retired life. He had never married. So, there were no kids whom he knew of. He could never find a woman, who matched him mentally, or intellectually. This was the reason for him not to marry.

In Eddington, he started getting back to his bike trips, mountaineering, cliff hanging, swimming, canoeing, sky diving, horse riding. The only sex Prince knew was casual sex or one-night stands. He could never stand the same women for a long time.

Because of his astonishing good looks and adventurous lifestyle, he never had a dearth of good-looking women. The aimless adventure and sex, even at the age of 60+ started taking its toll. By late 2012, he was bored, looking for an adventure like earlier times. He still had tremendous contacts within the global spy agencies.

By July 2013 Ralph Stevens the CIA chief approached him for *'Project wall'*. The first year was disastrous. The project was coming out to be another mass destruction project, as major portion was allowed to be run by Pakistan ISI. It was only when Ranjit approached Prince, the things improved to Prince's liking.

Prince had been closely associated with Ranjit Singh, National Security Advisor of India. When Ranjit had a discussion with Prince and Ralph, Prince agreed to join the Indian project, of course with Ralph's approval.

Now, there were two projects for the same final goal. Ralph led Project wall with the help of MI8, ISI etc. The Prince started another project "Project Brihadratha", after the last Mauryan King.

Till end of 2017, the two projects worked together, with agents helping each other. However, after a few incidents, Prince separated Brihadratha, due to principal disagreements.

CHAPTER 11

Meeting The Prince

June 30, 2016. I had a meeting with The Prince in his office. I was told over the phone that someone will meet me in the parking lot of the Vayu Sena Bhavan.

As soon as I parked my car, a uniformed staff member approached me and silently gestured for me to follow him. He led me to the reception area, where a lady dressed in a professional business suit handed me a visitor's pass and motioned for me to follow her.

While waiting for the elevator, I couldn't help but notice that the lady had a fit and athletic physique. I found myself admiring her as we stood there. Being a sports enthusiast myself, I struck up a conversation and asked if she played any sports. She responded with a smile and shook her head, indicating that she didn't.

Curiosity got the better of me, and I wanted to continue our conversation by asking for her name. She softly murmured "Florence." I was about to confirm if I heard her correctly, but just then, the elevator arrived. Once inside, I took the opportunity to initiate the conversation again.

I admitted that I didn't know why I was there and asked if she had any knowledge about the purpose of the meeting. She assured me that she did but suggested that it would be better for The Prince to explain it to me personally. She mentioned that it would only take a few more minutes.

Realizing that Florence wouldn't be accompanying me for much longer, I couldn't help but appreciate her presence.

It had been a while since I had spent time with a woman, and her alluring scent and athletic physique were quite enticing. A few more moments with her would have been appreciated.

I still had no idea why I was in the building. However, with Florence by my side, I found myself seriously considering whatever opportunity was about to be presented to me.

To my surprise, when the elevator doors opened, we found ourselves on the tenth floor, which happened to be the top floor of the building. But instead of leading to another office space, the doors opened onto a beautiful lawn.

I had never seen a lawn on the tenth floor before, growing up in Delhi. The surrounding buildings weren't as tall, so we could see the old furniture and discarded items on their terraces. From there, we could even catch a glimpse of the India Gate in the distance.

After crossing the lawn, we entered the other section of the building. There was a single door that led to a spacious seating area, followed by a row of three or four cabins. Florence opened the door, and we stepped inside. I was directed towards an unmarked cabin and told to enter.

Inside, there was a man sitting at the head of the table. He was short, aged, and had a tanned complexion, yet he maintained an athletic physique. His stylishly thinning grey hair added to his overall appearance. He wore dark jeans and a dark blue Polo T-shirt. However, there was something about him that didn't quite match his polite demeanor. His eyes seemed to reveal a ruthless nature, someone who wouldn't hesitate to kill, even at the slightest provocation. He introduced himself as 'Prince', although I could guess it wasn't his real name.

The meeting was brief, but it was clear that Prince knew everything about me.

He didn't waste any time and immediately offered his condolences for my recent loss. He knew that both of my parents had passed away just a few days ago. He briefly mentioned my achievements, including my swimming days and how I narrowly missed winning a bronze medal in the 2010 Commonwealth Games. He even knew about my family, including my father's factory and his desire for me to join the family business, despite my decision to join the forces.

What caught me off guard were two remarks he made. First, he mentioned that now that my father was no longer here, it would be easier for me to decide on my future career.

This comment felt harsh and almost rude, especially considering the emotional state I was in after losing both of my parents.

While I was about to counter this remark, he made another statement, which made me dumbstruck. Prince told me that my brother wanted to own the family business 100%, and it would be better if I chose a different occupation.

How could he know that?

Although Mr. Tandon, my father's lawyer friend, had hinted at this to me. Coming from Prince, this looked creepy. I was pissed about these two statements; but I chose to keep quiet.

Seeing me quiet, without going into any further details, he asked if I would like to reconsider my decision to disregard the active life. If yes, he had an interesting job proposal for me.

I did not speak immediately. As had been trained in the forces, I first controlled my emotions and made an effort, not showing any, on my face.

After a deliberate pause, I told him, this was quite early, as I had still not come out of my bereavement.

Losing both parents on the same day, in such a tragic way, is a grief, which no one should experience. Also, I was still exploring my ways to be a civilian.

He comprehended. He served me tea and from then on, we conversed solely about my parents, brother, brother's wife, my niece, and their strong bond. It appeared to be a casual chat, but I later realized it was far from casual. The Prince was evaluating me. He was observing my actions and expressions; how connected I was to my remaining family.

Years later, I understood that it was a wise choice not to show that I was close to my brother and his family. Otherwise, their fate might have been different from what it is now. Little did I know then that a girl named Anita had already determined the path of my life.

On my way home, I couldn't stop pondering about the discussion, particularly the two comments The Prince made.

I had a feeling that my brother and his wife had become deeply involved in the family business. They aimed to have full control over it. Now that I was back, they realized they had to split the ownership equally with me.

Mr. Tandon had informed me about this. He shared a conversation he had with my brother after our parents' passing. My brother and his wife were willing to allocate only 20% in my favor. Mr. Tandon had also offered his support in case things turned sour.

Being single, I calculated that even 20% was sufficient for me. It was more than what I earned from my government job. Hence, it didn't bother me.

I also pondered if there was any underlying message in the discussion about my parents and the ease of my career decisions in their absence. At that time, I didn't detect any hidden implications.

It wasn't until many years later that I realized.

After returning from the agency office, the next day I had a discussion about the business with my brother. Since our parents had passed away without leaving a will, there was no question of any document deciding the share between the two of us.

My brother expressed his happiness for me joining the business, as it was our father's wish after all. However, I couldn't shake off the feeling that he might not truly want that.

He continued, "You must have become accustomed to a different lifestyle. Would you be interested in a stable nine-to-five job?"

I didn't respond, so he went on, "You know, if you want, you can continue doing something exciting for a little longer. I'll take care of the business and keep it ready for you when you feel ready for it."

Still, I didn't reply.

I knew that my brother's wife wanted her lazy brother to become a shareholder in our business. My father had hinted at this during our last meeting, and he had firmly refused. Taking this into consideration, I spoke up. "Let's create an agreement where we are equal partners. I won't take a single penny until I am working elsewhere. However, the day I return, we can start sharing the profits."

My brother glanced at his wife and then continued, "We'll have to include Sneha (his wife) as a shareholder in the agreement as well."

I pondered for a moment. So, what about my future wife, if I marry?

I took some time to respond, using that time to analyze my current situation. I had no interest in a static job, and it was frustrating to me. The offer from Prince was also tempting. However, I didn't want to let go of what my father had decided for me.

After a brief pause, I calmly stated, "That's okay. You both can keep 60% for yourselves, I'm fine with 40%." It was a generous offer on my part, as I willingly gave up not only my 10%, but also the majority or equal partnership rights without any hesitation.

When Sneha suggested her brother become an additional partner, I firmly declined. I emphasized that it should remain a family matter within the Sharma family.

I proposed that this clause be included in our partnership agreement as a Sharma family concern. There would be a separate agreement outlining the company's assets and our parents' belongings, which would be divided equally between my brother and me. Despite Sneha's apparent dissatisfaction, we reached a final decision.

Once everything was settled, I contacted Mr. Tandon. The following day, he arrived with the new partnership agreement and property rights settlement. He seemed pleased that we were able to resolve everything without outside assistance. When he inquired if I was satisfied with the division, I assured him that I was content even if my brother ended up with 100%.

My main priority was to have a say in the business and ensure that it remained a family affair. Mr. Tandon presented the agreements, which were signed by me, my brother, and Sneha. He notarized them and provided each of us with a copy.

With this matter resolved, I made the decision to explore the offer from The Prince. Although I wasn't entirely sure what it entailed, I anticipated that it would be an exciting opportunity despite my limited experience.

I made a call to Prince's office the following day and requested an appointment. The call happened to be on July 5th, which also coincided with my birthday.

It was quite an emotional day for me, especially since my mother used to insist on taking me to the temple on my birthdays. Despite my resistance, she would always urge me to go.

Today was different. I missed her presence dearly and decided to visit the temple on my own for the first time.

As I knelt down in the temple, tears streamed down my face. I couldn't help but wonder why both my parents were taken away from me. I had promised to be there for them always, and if I had known their time was limited, I would have never left.

Lost in my emotions, the priest approached me and gently placed his hand on my head. He allowed me to cry and then comforted me by saying that my parents were with God. He encouraged me to visit the temple frequently, assuring me that I would feel their presence.

It took some time for me to compose myself, but once I did, I made a promise to God that I would accept whatever Prince offered me that day. It was my way of distancing myself from my current frustrations and contributing something meaningful to the country.

I arrived at Prince's office promptly at 10:30. Having been there before, I knew what to expect. However, to my surprise, Florence was nowhere to be found. Instead, a tall and stout man greeted me.

Standing at six and a half feet, he made me feel like a dwarf, despite being over six feet tall myself. He escorted me to the elevator, and we made our way to meet Prince.

The elevator ride was uneventful, but it was during our walk on the office lawns, overlooking the magnificent view, that the giant man welcomed me to the agency and assured me that I wouldn't regret joining.

I couldn't help but feel that the agency's decisions and business were not as confidential as I had initially thought. First, Florence seemed to know why I was here, and now this bulky man. It seemed like everyone was aware of my purpose.

And, by the way, how on earth did he know that I had accepted the offer? First, I had to know the offer, then I would have made up my mind.

This second meeting with Prince lasted for approximately one hour. Prince began by warmly welcoming me to the agency. Still in a state of shock, I couldn't help but express my surprise. To my astonishment, he replied, "I had a feeling you would join."

The next thirty minutes were dedicated to introducing me to the work I would be doing for the agency.

I had anticipated some bureaucratic paperwork to formalize my joining, but to my surprise, there was none. Prince continued to speak, and I was expected to absorb everything he said.

Prince explained, "To complete your joining formalities, you just need to sign a few documents. There is a detailed list of rules and regulations that you will sign, and you will receive a copy for your reference. Take your time to read it, commit it to memory, and then destroy it. It must not be kept in existence."

"Please provide a list of your former colleagues and friends who have your phone number, and we will ensure that they never contact you again. Their records will mysteriously lose your number and address."

"You will still be able to communicate with your brother and other family members whenever you or they desire. However, all conversations will be recorded and monitored. Regardless of the phone number you use, your current number will appear on their phones. They will never know your location or new numbers."

Prince continued, "Next, you will be traveling to London for a month of training. We are aware of your exceptional combat training and physical fitness, which make you perfect for the assignments ahead. This training will introduce you to the work expected from you."

"All the arrangements have been made. I understand that you do not currently possess a UK Visa. However, by July 20th, you will have a new diplomatic passport and visa. You will report to India House in London and be introduced as a personal security assistant to a diplomatic attaché."

"You must be curious about the end goal, right? Currently, our focus is on building a more prosperous, powerful, and economically advanced India. Your team and you will play a crucial role in achieving this".

"When you arrive in London, you will discover more. For now, please refrain from asking questions as this is all I can reveal at the moment. Ganesh (pointing to the giant) will assist you in getting settled and will guide you further".

Wow. That's how I was excused from the meeting. That's how I became part of the agency. Was I really certain about joining the agency?

It took me another 15 minutes to complete the signing of the neatly typed agreement, which left me feeling puzzled. I was handed a copy containing a detailed list of confidentiality instructions, which I was supposed to review on my way home and then destroy before reaching my destination.

As I journeyed back, unanswered questions lingered in my mind. How can we ensure a better, stronger, and economically stable India from London?

One question that I didn't ponder on at that moment was whether I was actually joining the Indian government agency. This realization only hit me five years later.

Reflecting on the statement "we'll ensure they never contact you (your number and address will mysteriously vanish from their records)", a chilling thought crossed my mind. If these individuals were so influential, should my family or I be concerned?

Another fleeting thought arose - was my parents' accident truly an accident? Perhaps this stemmed from my disbelief that my father could drive so recklessly on a foggy night, knowing the risks involved.

When I considered things rationally, I doubted that the government would go to such extreme lengths just to secure my services, especially when India had highly skilled and dedicated individuals in the police force.

What did I really know?

As I was told by The Prince, I travelled to London during last week of July 2016. I had told my brother that I had rejoined the forces and was posted in the Andamans.

I landed at India House as a personal security officer to Mr. Ramesh Lal, finance attaché at Indian embassy. I was chosen to be with Mr. Lal, as the primary requirement of my job was to know what happened in the global financial circles. As Mr. Lal could attend all such meetings, I, as his security officer, could get the proceedings recorded.

The advantage the PSOs have is they are never frisked for the recording devices. They can carry two-way communication devices with them, which they are required to carry for their bosses. The said communication devices can very well be modified as recording devices as well.

While the spy world knows about this, they can do nothing to safeguard against this, as every country needs to secure their diplomats, and also, every country needs the information.

I started my work in London as PSO to Mr. Lal. For the agency work, Prince introduced me with a man called Jon Russel, in August of 2016.

CHAPTER

The agency

The agency was founded in India in 1965, with Mr. Ram Narayan Jain serving as its first Director. Mr. Rishi Nayyar was appointed as the assistant director and was also responsible for the personal security of India's first Prime Minister.

Although Mr. Jain held the position of the agency's first Director, Mr. Nayyar is widely regarded as the father of India's external Intelligence agency. He assumed the role of Director in 1968 and remained in command until 1977.

During Mr. Nayyar's tenure, India faced numerous security threats both internally and externally. The world was grappling with a severe recession, leading to unrest, protests, invasions, and domestic violence. However, thanks to Mr. Nayyar's efforts, India managed to minimize the impact of these challenges.

Mr. Nayyar is also credited as the father of Bangladesh, as his sources provided India with crucial information about Pakistan's military operations. This inside knowledge played a significant role in shaping India's actions.

Rishi belonged to the 1945 batch of the Indian Police Service from the Gujarat cadre, but his entire career was spent in New Delhi on central assignments. He possessed an extraordinary blend of physical and mental prowess. However, he was modest when it came to discussing his own accomplishments, friends, and personal life.

Following the partition of India and Pakistan in 1947, Rishi, due to his youthful age, striking appearance, and polished demeanor, was entrusted with the responsibility of the Indian Prime Minister's personal security. He held this position until 1954, not only serving as a security advisor but also becoming a trusted confidant.

In 1954, he was transferred back to his home cadre of Gujarat but was soon called back to take charge of a highly sensitive intelligence operation.

The Chinese government had chartered an Air India aircraft named 'The Deccan Queen' for the Chinese Prime Minister, Chu Uang Lai, who was scheduled to attend the Bali Conference, flying from Hong Kong to Jakarta. However, at the last moment, the Chinese premier canceled his trip, citing excruciating appendicitis pain.

Tragically, the plane crashed near the Indonesian coast, resulting in the loss of many Chinese officials and journalists on board.

Rishi, with his insider knowledge, had informed the Indian Prime Minister in advance about probability of this incident. The information was passed on to the Chinese Prime Minister, who cancelled the trip.

It was thus natural that Rishi was given the task of delving into the incident. During his investigation, Rishi discovered the involvement of intelligence agency of Taiwan. He uncovered that a group of Taiwanese agents, disguised as journalists, had swapped the cameras of Chinese journalists with ones containing explosives and had abruptly canceled their trip at the last minute.

Prime Minister Lai was so impressed that he invited Rishi to his office and gifted him his personal seal as a token of appreciation. This seal remained on Rishi's desk until his retirement.

Prior to this event, India did not have an external intelligence agency, but this incident highlighted the necessity for such an organization for the first time.

From 1955 to 1963, the remaining years of India's first Prime Minister were marred by turmoil in India and the entire Southeast Asian region. It included an attack by China on India, which was the worst thanks China gave India, for saving China's premier's life.

During this period, China also took control of the Tibetan government. There were various revolts, uprisings, and assassination attempts in the region, including the USA's attack on Vietnam, which led to significant unrest in the area.

It was also during this time that the Indian Prime Minister fell seriously ill with an incurable disease, ultimately passing away in 1963. The second Indian Prime Minister died under mysterious circumstances in Tashkent.

Despite the absence of an external intelligence agency in India at that time, Rishi managed to gather information from his sources. This information revealed that the death of the second Indian premier was not a natural occurrence. Rishi had concrete evidence that the KGB was involved in this foul play.

When he shared this information with the potential new Prime Minister, he was offered a prestigious position of his choice in the new regime, possibly as a reward for his silence.

Surprisingly, the ruling party in India appointed a young lady as the new Prime Minister, assuming that they would have control over her due to her gender and age. Little did they know that this young lady would turn out to be one of the strongest leaders India had ever seen and would also establish a dynastic rule.

True to her promise to Rishi, the new Prime Minister decided to establish a foreign intelligence agency in India, similar to the CIA, KGB, and MI-8. Rishi was nominated to be its first director. But he was young, and junior compared to many others, who could not be superseded. Therefore, Mr. Jain was chosen as the first director, with Rishi serving as his deputy. In reality, Rishi was the one who effectively ran the agency, while Mr. Jain was merely a figurehead.

The 1971 India-Pakistan war showcased Rishi's invaluable contributions. His men played a crucial role in training over one lakh Mukti Bahini soldiers from East Pakistan under his careful guidance. Interestingly, this training exercise was intentionally leaked to the Pakistan army, provoking them to launch an attack on East Pakistan and India.

The consequences of this attack were detrimental for Pakistan, resulting in their defeat and the creation of Bangladesh, formerly known as East Pakistan.

India had to approach this war strategically due to Pakistan's presence on both its eastern and western borders. Thankfully, the prime minister possessed sharp intellect, and she had the support of equally sharp officers in the Army and Intelligence agency.

The Indian Army General and Rishi shared a close friendship, and together they devised a brilliant master plan.

According to the terms agreed upon during the partition of India, Pakistan had the right to use Indian airspace, even for military aircraft, at all times. This was a continuous threat to Indian security.

However, there was a specific clause in the agreement that allowed India to halt this usage if Pakistan's aggression threatened India's security.

Although the Pakistani government was aware that the Mukti Bahini had received training from the Indian intelligence agency, they couldn't risk attacking India.

Doing so would have led to the suspension of Indian airspace usage, which would have been disastrous for them in suppressing the Mukti Bahini uprising in East Pakistan. On the contrary, India desired aggression to justify blocking the airspace.

Here is, how Rishi gamed Pakistan.

He knew the movement of every Pakistani agent in this region. One day, he got an information that a few agents would be travelling on an Indian Airlines Civil aircraft, to Dhaka in East Pakistan. The flight had to take off from Karachi in Pakistan, had a stopover at Amritsar, then Delhi and then Dhaka.

When the aircraft landed at Amritsar, two Kashmiri men boarded the plane. When the plane took off, they took out the guns they were carrying and highjacked the plane. The plane was then forced to land at Srinagar airport.

Here, to the utter surprise of the Pakistani agents, the hijackers demanded release of three Pakistani captives in Indian jails. The Indian forces continued the negotiations for a few hours. When the hijackers were little drowsy, Indian forces forcefully entered the plane and took them under their control. The hijackers started speaking in Urdu with Pakistani agents, calling them their superiors. All of them were taken into custody.

In the evening the same day, Indian government announced the blocking of airspace for Pakistani aircrafts, till the pendency of the hijacking incident investigation.

While the Pakistani agents were taken to Srinagar jail, the hijackers were seen having tea at Oberoi Lakeview hotel in Srinagar. They were to go on a long holiday, before preparing for their next mission. For the newspapers, the hijackers were identified as Pakistani citizens, accompanying the agents, who were sentenced to ten-year imprisonment along with Pakistani agents.

Pakistan attacked East Pakistan to suppress Mukti Bahini and in turn India. The war lasted for 18 days and ended with emergence of Bangladesh. Pakistan lost heavily, lost many of its soldiers, self-esteem, and the eastern side of Pakistani land.

The agency under Rishi, also had a tremendous role in the merger of Sikkim with India.

Sikkim remained an independent state till 1971, like Nepal. The Sikkim problem started when its ruler married an American woman. The lady he married was a CIA agent. Soon, American interference started in Sikkim.

Given Sikkim's strategic location at the border of India and China, America wanted to establish its presence and control. The world had already seen the damage America had done in Vietnam, where again, it wanted its presence and control.

The skirmish was now tripartite. America wanted its presence to control India and China, China never wanted

America's presence and India of course wanted access to its eastern territories called the seven sisters.

As Sikkim was strategically located on the eastern side of India, had China or America been able to assume the charge, India would have been completely cut off by road, with its north-east states, Assam, Meghalaya, Nagaland, Mizoram, Manipur, Tripura and Arunachal Pradesh.

Being aware about the geopolitical situation, Rishi suggested to Indian PM, that he could help Sikkim merge with India. Once the Indian PM provided the desired nod, within days, Sikkim became a part of India in a bloodless coup. This all happened right under the nose of China and the American CIA agent, who happened to be the wife of Sikkim's ruler.

Rishi carried out this work with the help of only four officers. So much secrecy was maintained in this whole mission that apart from these four officers and of course, Indian Premier, none knew anything.

Rishi was aware about debauchery of the Sikkim's ruler. Despite his new marriage to the CIA agent, the ruler was introduced to a stunning northeastern beauty, who made the ruler fall in love with her, just after one night of steaming sex. During this night, this beauty did things to the ruler, which were unimaginable and unheard of.

Of course, everything was recorded on hidden video cameras. So, when the Chinese forces were on the border of Sikkim, the ruler was advised by this beauty to seek refuge with India, else the entire recording would be made available to new wife and of course would be displayed publicly.

Having no choice, the ruler signed on dotted lines, handing over the entire area of 3000 square kilometers of Sikkim to Indian government.

Sikkim became the 22nd state of India.

The Indian prime minister had become the unquestioned leader of all of South Asia. This sense of power went to her head and had negative consequences. She began surrounding herself with "yes-men" within the government.

By 1975, it became clear to the prime minister that the past few years had been disastrous. If there had been an election, she would have been voted out of power. In response, she started imprisoning opposition leaders on frivolous charges.

However, despite these actions, she still lost the elections.

The new prime minister, who took office in January 1976. He was from the opposition and suspected that Rishi played a significant role in the previous prime minister's mistreatment of the opposition. As a result, the new prime minister distanced himself from Rishi and initiated an internal investigation into his actions.

Rishi was ultimately cleared of any wrongdoing, but the agency suffered greatly during his suspension. The backup who managed the agency in Rishi's absence was not as capable, leading to the loss of around 50 assets. Some were compromised and killed, while others went rogue. The next two years were the agency's darkest period, with nobody willing to take risks.

In 1978, when Rishi said his final farewell to the agency, he was far from being a contented man.

Over the course of the last two years, a staggering 27 of his closest agents had lost their lives. These agents had been entrusted with the crucial task of uncovering the exact location in Pakistan where the country was secretly developing a nuclear bomb.

The journey had begun back in 1973 when they first caught wind of Pakistan's plans to build the nuke. From that moment on, Rishi's team tirelessly pursued every lead that came their way. They dispersed themselves throughout Pakistan, blending into various low-level jobs to maintain their cover.

While it took Pakistan two long years to successfully develop the nuclear weapon, the agents spent the same amount of time relentlessly searching for any clues that could lead them to the truth. There were moments when their operation seemed futile, and it was even called off twice due to the lack of concrete evidence.

However, it was Rajat, working inconspicuously at a hair cutting salon in Quetta, who made a breakthrough in November 1975. He sent some hair samples for examination, and to everyone's astonishment, they contained traces of radioactive material. This discovery provided the much-needed evidence to bring joy to New Delhi.

By December 25th, Rajat, along with his assistant Divya, who ran a tea shop from the same location, managed to trace the origin of the radioactive traces to a closed distillery. Every day, they observed the movement of certain individuals within the premises who appeared to be security guards, although their behavior was far from typical.

The presence of around 30 security guards in a closed distillery raised suspicions. Rajat and Divya had adopted new identities, Arshad and Samina, respectively. During holidays, the "guards" would occasionally order tea from their stall. It was on Christmas day in 1975 when Samina took tea to the guards. Little did they know, she was wearing a watch equipped with an inbuilt Dosimeter, capable of instantly detecting radioactivity.

When Divya returned to the stall, her face was just as radiant as the dosimeter. The watch's radioactivity reading indicated the presence of a nuclear weapon, confirming the existence of a bomb in the distillery.

The news was shared with Rishi that same night through a secret message. However, since the Indian prime minister had already lost the elections, they had to wait before sharing the information with the new government.

Rishi informed the new Prime Minister about the news on January 20, 1976. By February 5th, he was suspended and placed under investigation.

It was never proven who leaked the news, but starting from February 1976, the Indian agents responsible for tracking Pakistan's nuclear program began dying one by one.

It all began with Sarabhpreet, also known as Md. Imran, who died from food poisoning. Next was Rajat, also known as Arshad, was shot dead while he was having dinner in a local shop.

Samina managed to escape to Dubai on the same night Arshad was killed. She then kept moving from Iran to Muscat and Doha, but eventually she was killed during a failed robbery at her apartment in London in September 1976.

While the world now knew about Pakistan's nuclear program, the 26 out of 27 members of the team responsible for this significant discovery were martyred, without any recognition for their great work.

Pakistan had named this operation 'Gulfam'. The only agent who survived this elimination was Ranjit Singh, who now took it upon himself to seek revenge for his fallen teammates.

Ranjit, at 24 years old, was the youngest member of the team. He was an IPS officer from the Karnataka Cadre, belonging to the 1972 batch. This was his first official assignment, which taught him a valuable lesson for life.

It took Ranjit 12 years to eliminate each person responsible for the deaths of the 26 martyrs. The revenge finally came to an end when the Pakistani dictator, who was accountable for the deaths of the 26 agents, perished in a plane crash along with his closest aides, who carried out his orders.

Ranjit had received his training from Rishi. While Rishi exuded politeness, sophistication, and impeccable style, Ranjit was the complete opposite. His speech was rough and common. He could easily be mistaken for a fruit vendor, laborer, rickshaw puller, or any other blue-collar worker. He immersed himself in his work, embodying the persona he had crafted for himself.

Fluent in Punjabi, Pashto, Urdu, Kashmiri, Sindhi, and various other languages, Ranjit's linguistic skills proved to be a valuable asset in his endeavors, always benefiting India.

In the world of intelligence, agents often find themselves isolated, living in the made-up reality they have constructed for their missions.

This was no different for Ranjit, who, at a young age, lost his entire team. Cutting off all communication with his superiors, he was presumed dead until 1986.

CHAPTER

Ranjit Singh

Born as the only child in a Sikh business family in Ladiya Kalan, near Ludhiana, Punjab, in 1949, Ranjit Singh had a very safe and secure childhood. His future was secure financially, as his family were rich and honorable in the area.

As the tradition went in the family, he was supposed to complete his initial education and join the family business.

So, before he turned 16, he was asked to attend the family hosiery mill, in Ladiya Kalan itself. The mill was manufacturing woolen knitwear and had a steady supply order from Indian Army and paramilitary forces.

Ranjit's father was the youngest amongst the four brothers. The mill was started by his grandfather, who still managed all the affairs of business. Being the youngest amongst all the cousins, Ranjit was considered the baby of the house. He was sharp in studies unlike his cousins, who treated him as a nerd, still being proud of him.

One day, timidly, Ranjit asked his father if he could complete his graduation. His father permitted him reluctantly.

So, Ranjit joined Government College, Ludhiana to pursue graduation. The distance to his college from the family home was some ten kilometers, so he was given a motor bike to commute.

He graduated in 1970, at the age of 21 and topped the entire Punjab university.

When Ranjit proposed to his father that he wanted to pursue his masters, considering Ranjit's grades, his father could not say no. Although his cousins teased him that he wanted to pursue education to be with girls, they respected his passion for studies and nicknamed him Gyani (learned man).

One day, when Ranjit came home, he saw a crowd of people at home. His grandfather had passed away. His parents and entire family were gathered in the porch, while relatives and friends kept pouring in to pay their last respects. For the next ten days, the mill remained closed, as the family was in mourning.

Soon thereafter, started a tussle between his uncles and father for succession. Grandfather had died without a will. While his father and younger uncles wanted an equal share in the business, his eldest uncle was not in favor. He wanted to run the mill, just as their father was running.

He expected that his younger siblings would pay him the same respect, while he decides on sharing of profits.

The eldest uncle had three sons, who were all married and matured in rustic way. The younger two uncles had two daughters each, all married and settled in their respective homes. The reason for asking for equal share was, as everyone wanted a fair share for the next generation. But the rift continued.

One evening, when he returned home, he saw his parents sitting on the porch.

Apparently, there had been a fight amongst the uncles and his father, and his father was asked by the uncles to leave the house. His male cousins also joined in and threatened that Ranjit would be killed.

As Ranjit was the only male heir in the house after his uncles and three male cousins, he was the threat to inheritance for his cousins.

Being the studious one, Ranjit was never interested in being tough. His parents were worried for his safety, as they knew, in a fight, Ranjit would definitely give up.

His father was equally disturbed that his elder brothers did not support and had sided with the eldest brother, in this dispute. Having no support, the same night, they left the house and stayed with Ranjit's maternal uncle, who stayed in Ludhiana.

Ranjit's father had some savings. He started some trading business. But now it was important for Ranjit to do something for his life.

He appeared for various competitive exams for government jobs. He also applied for civil services. The luck favored the hard-working lad, and he got selected on the first attempt, into Indian Police Service.

All of this took around a year. As earnings of Ranjit's father were not sufficient, Ranjit worked part time to provide the family with something respectful.

Soon, it was time for Ranjit to go for basic training. He was concerned for his parents, but his father pushed him to go. Financially, there was no need for Ranjit to worry for himself, as during the training, he was to be provided enough stipend to support himself. He was more worried about his parents, as during the next thirteen months, they were to survive on meager commissions, which his father earned through trading of hosiery.

During the entire training, Ranjit was an average cadet. He was still not physically tough, but cracked all the indoor exams, with top marks. He remained aloof from other trainees and kept to himself most of the time. He kept sending part of his stipend home, so his parents did not have to worry about money.

This was the first IPS batch with a few lady officers. Ranjit was doing fairly well in indoor exams; the girls tried their charm for his notes for the exams.

There was this girl, who fancied Ranjit, or at least Ranjit felt that way. Her name was Sukhbir Kaur. She was from Himachal and was an ace basketball player. Being a sports person, she was physically tough.

One evening she cornered Ranjit outside the officers' mess and took him towards the parade ground, which was secluded at that time. This is when Ranjit lost his virginity.

Thereafter, Ranjit continued coaching the girl, with mutual benefits of pleasure.

During the half yearly exams, Sukhbir stood first, Ranjit a close second. Still, Ranjit did not mind, as he looked forward to marrying Sukhbir.

It was sometime during the second half of the training, when Rishi visited the National Police Academy to scout for talent.

He stayed for a few days, observing each cadet closely. He narrowed down to some seven cadets. Of course, Ranjit topped the list due to his interpersonal behavior and looks.

In this group of seven, there was one girl, Divya Lal, and the rest all men. From now onwards, these seven cadets, got two extra classes each day, on surveillance and collecting intelligence.

It was also during this second half of the training; the cadets were allotted their respective state cadres. Ranjit got Karnataka, as his cadre. Sukhbir got Maharashtra.

During this time, Ranjit started realizing that Maharashtra cadre was managed by Sukhbir, as she was not ready to commit to marriage at that age. They could have managed to get their cadre changed and work in either Maharashtra or Karnataka cadre together, if they decided to get married, but this was not what Sukhbir wanted.

However, till the end of the training, they were considered a couple. They spent each minute of their free time, together. Once they passed out of the academy, the existence of each other was nearly forgotten.

Being this the first batch with lady officers, the academy director wanted a lady parade commander at the passing out parade. Sukhbir was the natural choice. She had topped in the indoor exams, she was physically fit, her firing points were much above others.

Although her parade was average, but the trainers were tasked to get that improved during passing out practice. They had a terrible time getting that done, but somehow, by final rehearsal, Sukhbir was much tolerable.

By now, it was clear that Ranjit would go to the secret service. His cadre remained as Karnataka, but he was to join on central deputation from the next day of passing out.

The other six officers, who were to join him, became good friends. They all admired the logic presented by Ranjit for each issue. It was as if he was meant for this work only.

Ranjit liked the admiration and during this time, knowing that Sukhbir was not interested in marrying him, concentrated more on getting physical pleasure with her.

Then came the passing out day. They all were dressed in starched, stiff cotton uniforms. Shoes shining, smartly filed in, at the parade ground. The passing out ceremony took some 90 minutes and at the end, parents of the cadets put the pips on their shoulders.

It was a proud moment for Ranjit's parents. They had come specially for this ceremony from Ludhiana. Ranjit made it a point that they do not meet Sukhbir's parents.

Evening came. There was much fan fair. The academy had organized some cultural dances for the entertainment of parents and visitors, followed by dinner at the officers' mess. Sukhbir met Ranjit and offered goodbye sex.

What the heck? Ranjit agreed. The new officers and their parents were seated separately. No one noticed the absence of Ranjit and Sukhbir during the dance presentations.

It was September 1973. Just out of the National Police Academy, Ranjit was supposed to spend three months for practical training at his parent cadre in Karnataka before he was sent on a mission abroad. His Kannada became fluent, but his ultimate aim was something else.

It was the first week of January 1974, when he was placed in Pakistan. His six friends from the academy joined in from their respective state cadres for this mission.

Divya was from Tamil Nādu Cadre and was named Samina. She was the one, who was successful in detecting the radioactive traces at Quetta, she was the one who got killed as Samina in London in 1976. Why did Ranjit survive and not the others? Only because of the logic he was famous for.

Although Ranjit was 24 at that time of his posting in Pakistan, he looked quite young. Since his childhood, he had learnt Urdu from a nearby maulvi, at Ladiya Kalan. He could read and write it fluently.

Communication in local language was not a problem for Ranjit in Pakistan since Punjabi, which was his mother tongue, was widely spoken there. During his two-year stay in the country, Ranjit, now known as Shahbaz Alam, constantly changed jobs and locations but made sure to maintain close relationships with local maulvis wherever he went.

He continuously acquired new skills, working at a spinning lathe factory in Lahore, as a die caster in Bahawalpur, and finally as a puncture man in Quetta. While in Lahore, he became acquainted with Zaira, a prostitute from Hira Mandi, who was being harassed by her pimp.

Ranjit came to Zaira's rescue once, and afterwards she expressed her desire to stay with him. Seeking a companion to establish his legitimacy in Pakistan, Ranjit allowed her to stay.

Throughout the next two years, he never lost contact with the maulvis, understanding that they were trusted by Muslims for always speaking the truth. His network remained intact.

Ranjit remained with Zaira, although she wanted to marry and have children, which he always avoided. Eventually, Zaira had enough and decided to leave Ranjit one night, causing a scene at their house. The entire area became aware of their separation due to the commotion, but it didn't matter to Ranjit.

The following day, Ranjit quit his job and relocated to Bahawalpur. He never altered his story of being an orphan who grew up near Lahore Railway station. He never appeared in public with any other agents and communicated with Indian intelligence officers solely through post, using different languages in his written correspondence.

He learned Pashto from the Pathan who owned the lathe workshop, Kashmiri from a fellow worker, and Sindhi from a clothes trader, whom he worked for as a porter.

He was 27 years old when the team massacre began. He was never suspected of being one of them, because of his carefully crafted background. The sources, who kept informing the Pakistani secret agents about the Indian agents, never considered Ranjit to be one of the Indian secret agents. They had already confirmed his story with Maulvis in Lahore, Bahawalpur, and Quetta.

At the time his team was killed, he was running a puncture repair shop in Quetta. Unfazed, Ranjit continued with the same business for the next two months, ensuring no contact with the agency. He knew that if he made any moves during that time, he would be under surveillance.

In the third month, he left Quetta claiming to search for better job opportunities and returned to his previous employer in Lahore. He claimed that he had earned enough money by then.

His former employer had a lathe factory and a bicycle shop. He also had three daughters and four sons. The sons were known goons and never worked. So, Ranjit offered some money to become a partner in the bicycle business.

Soon, the old employer offered to sell the shop to him for a substantial amount of money. Ranjit had a large sum of agency money safely hidden at a secluded place. He purchased the shop and started managing it full-time.

He began using the hidden money to expand his business further and to seek revenge.

He was regularly involved in a sexual relationship with Kubra, the youngest daughter of his old employer. One evening, he was caught in the act by one of Kubra's brothers.

By this time, Ranjit was considered financially stable. The next morning, a Maulvi was called, who arranged for Ranjit to marry Kubra.

This is not what Ranjit wanted, but danger still looming on his head, he got married anyway.

Ranjit's life took a turn for the better within the next three months. His earnings started to increase, thanks to his good behavior.

In June 1977, he was awarded the agency of Sohrab bicycles, which led to an increase in his business and trips. He had established reliable sources in Pakistan who provided him with valuable information about the ISI. By September, he obtained the entire list of ISI agents involved in the massacre of Indian agents.

Ranjit decided to embark on longer road trips, now that he had bought a Honda CD70 Motorcycle. To ensure his safety and anonymity, he would park his bike at the railway station or airport late at night, change the number plates and his appearance, and then follow the lead to his next target. The following day, he would change his appearance again and return home to celebrate his successful mission with Kubra, enjoying their time together.

Being in a Muslim country made it easier for Ranjit to change his appearance. He could assume various identities such as a maulvi, a Peer (saint), a Pathan, or even a woman in a burka. He carefully selected his targets, ensuring they were alone before making his move. With no CCTV cameras in those days, he never worried about getting caught. It took Ranjit a considerable amount of time to eliminate all those involved in the massacre of Indian agents.

Ranjit had already experienced many ups and downs in his life. Despite being born into an affluent Punjabi family, there were still days when they struggled to make ends meet. He excelled in Police training, but his heart was broken by his first love. While he continued to perform well in his job, he tragically lost his entire team without any recognition.

By September 1977, armed with the entire list of ISI executioners, and having enough resources, Ranjit started his revenge journey.

Since February 1976, he had severed all ties with the Indian agency. Unsure of who was a friend and who was a foe, Ranjit found solace in his three-year stay in Pakistan. It provided him with the resources necessary for his quest for revenge.

But his mission held a deeper purpose - his own survival. Ranjit understood that as long as even a single ISI agent involved in project Gulfam remained alive, there was a chance of him being discovered. To ensure his own safety, the executioners had to be eliminated.

The elimination began.

Mushtaq

At the top of his list was Mushtaq Ansari, also known as Jameel.

In 1977, ISI launched operation 'Game Friday' to gather intelligence on Pakistani Communist fundamentalists. With the Soviet Afghan war coming to a close, individuals with Communist beliefs began to settle from Kajura in Afghanistan to Landi Kotal in Peshawar.

The journey from Kajura to Landi Kotal was about 110 kilometers, taking just over two hours by car. However, since these migrants were illegal, they had to travel on foot, hiding in the hilly terrain. Border crossings into Pakistan was not difficult, as the Kabul riverbed was not closely monitored.

The Kabul river flows from Kabul and Jalalabad in Afghanistan, north of the Khyber Pass into Pakistan, and past Peshawar before joining the Indus River northwest of Islamabad. To reach Khyber Pakhtunkhwa in Pakistan, the illegal migrants would take a bus to Laalpur, then ride makeshift boats to Ghilzo Mena. From there, they would walk along the riverbed about 500 meters into Durma Kor in Khyber Pakhtunkhwa, Pakistan.

The area was home to ancient Buddhist caves, providing a natural hiding spot for the migrants. Once in Khyber Pakhtunkhwa, they could easily blend in with the local population, as Pashto was spoken throughout this region of Afghanistan and Pakistan.

The people in Peshawar shared similar features with Afghans, making it even easier for the immigrants to assimilate. Peshawar, being a more economically stable district compared to Afghanistan, attracted these immigrants who had been influenced by Communist ideologies taught by the Soviets for a long time.

Peshawar, also known as the city of flowers, is the oldest city in Pakistan and shares a similar landscape with most of Afghanistan. It was once called 'Purushpura' and served as the capital of the Kushan Empire under the rule of Kanishka. The city was home to the magnificent Kanishka stupa, one of the tallest structures in the ancient world. With a recorded history dating back to at least 539 BCE, Peshawar is one of the oldest cities in South Asia and has been continuously inhabited since then.

Peshawar has always been renowned for its natural beauty, both in terms of its geography and its people. The men and women of Peshawar are known for their tall stature, broad shoulders, sharp features and confidence. The city is blessed with lush green fields that are always adorned with beautiful flowers. These flowers are exported worldwide, contributing to the city's economic independence and the prosperity of its citizens.

According to Ranjit's sources, Mushtaq worked as a scholar and Head of the Department of Urdu, in Islamia College University in Peshawar. His job at the college was the front, while his main job for ISI was understanding the Afghani Communists and their ideologies and restrict their advancement.

One pleasant morning in September 1977, Ranjit expressed his desire to Kubra, to explore the Hunza Valley on his motorbike. This newfound passion of Ranjit's was greatly admired by Kubra.

Ranjit had joined a select group of bikers, which was considered quite exclusive and prestigious at that time. Kubra was delighted as their family gained popularity due to Ranjit's unique hobby. Ranjit had even purchased a luxurious Honda motorbike to enhance his biking experience.

Kubra, being well-versed with the business, had no trouble managing the shop in Ranjit's absence.

The distance between Lahore and Hunza was approximately 1000 KMs, but Ranjit and his new group decided to take a detour to Peshawar, adding an extra 200 KMs each way. Their twelve-day tour plan included three days to reach Peshawar, two-day stay there, and one day of travel to Hunza. They planned to spend two days in Hunza and kept two days for the return journey to Lahore. They also set aside an additional day for any unexpected situations.

However, what they didn't inform their spouses, was their purpose for visiting Peshawar.

Certain areas in Peshawar, such as Hayatabad, Islamabad bazaar, and Thatti bazar, were known to be accessible only to the wealthy. These places were popular among the rich and elite for entertainment. For a few hundred rupees, one could enjoy live music performed by talented female singers throughout the day and night, with additional services available if desired.

The group was excited about this prospect, but Ranjit had something else in mind. He had planned a painful fate for Mushtaq.

During their 52-hour stay in Peshawar, Ranjit spent most of his time visiting Islamia College University.

On his first visit, with the help of a student, Ranjit located Mushtaq's office from a distance. The university building displayed a beautiful blend of Islamic Mughal architecture. The grand structure featured domes, kiosks adorned with cupolas, and ornate pinnacles and finials, creating a captivating sight. As an ancient building, the rooms were spacious with high ceilings, providing a cool environment.

The room where Mushtaq had an office, was on the first floor, just below the clock tower, overlooking the mosque. Ranjit noticed that while the university campus was deserted after 4:00 PM, the HODs stayed, usually till six.

There was construction going on, which made it easier for Ranjit to plan and carry out his execution of Mushtaq. To confirm Mushtaq's identity, he entered the room and glanced at the nameplate that read Mushtaq Ansari, HOD, in Urdu.

The following day, Ranjit left his hotel with a mischievous glimmer in his eye, informing his biker friends that he was going to visit a woman. He parked his bike outside the 300-acre university, entered the premises, and changed into a worker's attire. He covered his head with a Pakul, a soft rolled-up Peshawari cap.

Ranjit packed a large, sharp chisel and a hammer in his tool bag, along with other tools. Since construction was underway, no one found his presence suspicious. He located the electrical main switch on the first floor and, at around four thirty PM, turned it off.

Exactly ten minutes later, Ranjit stood outside Mushtaq's room, holding a screwdriver, requesting permission to inspect the switchboard. Once granted entry, he closed the door behind him.

The corridor was empty, so he wasn't concerned about anyone walking in. He approached the switchboard, situated behind Mushtaq's desk. Pretending to inspect, he tapped on the switches.

When Mushtaq turned towards his desk, Ranjit swiftly pulled out the hammer and struck him on the head.

Mushtaq lost consciousness and slumped face down on his desk. Ranjit gently turned Mushtaq's head on the desk, retrieved the sharp, long chisel, and began hammering it into the left temporal area. The chisel was so sharp that it only took three blows for it to emerge from the right temporal area. With one final strike, he secured the head to the wooden desk.

Ranjit took precautions to ensure his clothes remained unstained by blood. He had placed a file between himself and Mushtaq to prevent any blood splatter. However, his hands were soaked, which he cleaned in a water jug. Before leaving the room, he meticulously wiped down all the tools, switchboard, the jug, the desk, and anything else he had touched.

DNA tracing was not yet invented, so he had no chance of getting caught.

He knew Mushtaq's murder would be investigated by ISI, so, he had already planned an alibi.

He left the room and the university, changing to a clean shirt in one of the deserted rooms. Took his bike and visited Nargis house in Hayatabad. Nusrat Jahan, who owned the house, was an old contact, who provided a young girl for Ranjit and an alibi, that he remained in Nargis house throughout the day.

Next for about an hour, Ranjit and the girl were locked in the room.

When Ranjit and the group left for Hunza the next morning, the ISI investigation into the murder of Mushtaq had already begun. There were no eyewitnesses.

Although the ISI believed this to be the work of a professional, they could never trace the murderer.

Nimma

After successfully completing his first mission, Ranjit felt motivated to pursue his next target. This time, it was Naeem Kausar, also known as Nimma, who Ranjit had decided should meet an untimely end. Nimma was responsible for the deaths of Rajat, Rakesh, and later Divya. Compared to Mushtaq, Nimma was an easier target since he had retired and settled in Dubai.

Intelligence circles were well aware of Nimma's active involvement in Dubai's underground party scene. There were even rumors that he supplied drugs, which carried a death penalty in Dubai.

Ranjit had a contact named Mohsin in Lahore who could arrange passports, visas, and other travel documents for those seeking jobs in the Middle East. Mohsin had a vast network of Pakistanis working in various professions such as cab drivers, house helps, and mechanics.

Once Ranjit got in touch with Mohsin, it took about 20 days to finalize the arrangements. When they met again, Mohsin provided confirmed details about Nimma's parties, the source of women for the guests, but he could not get details about the drugs. Mohsin also shared information about a caterer who managed the parties. This caterer was a Pakistani individual who had obtained "arranged" documentation through Mohsin's connections.

To avoid leaving any paper trail, Mohsin arranged a short two-day visit to Dubai for Ranjit using the "arranged" documents. During his trip, Ranjit met with Mohsin's contact and handed over audio and video recording devices to be discreetly used at Nimma's house.

Ranjit was aware that Nimma, being associated with ISI, would be familiar with such gadgets. Therefore, specific instructions were given to the contact on how to hide or camouflage the devices.

The recording devices were cleverly concealed within the music system, which the caterer would bring to the parties. As a result, Ranjit started receiving video and audio streams whenever there was a party at Nimma's house. He only had to wait for three parties before gathering enough evidence through the recordings. The evidence was clearly showing the regular supply of women, alcohol, and drugs at Nimma's residence.

The recordings had naked women smoking marijuana, while the men poured liquor on their bodies and drank. This was outright illegal in Dubai to be delt with death penalty.

Nimma diligently swept his house every day to ensure there were no bugs, especially after hosting parties. Therefore, he was completely taken aback when he discovered the Dubai Drug enforcement agency detectives at his doorstep one morning.

It turned out that two Dubai residents had become informants against Nimma, providing video and audio evidence of drugs being circulated at his parties. This act saved them from facing any consequences.

Tragically, Nimma was publicly executed in Dubai. The girls who were involved in his parties found themselves in the harem of the head of the enforcement agency, who also happened to be a Sheikh in Dubai.

Ranjit, aware that these two deaths would raise suspicions within the ISI, decided it was wise to take a break.

There were still six more people on his list.

During this time, Ranjit focused on growing his business. He successfully applied for a motorcycle agency and by March 1978, he was granted the agency for highly sought-after Derbi Bikes.

The opening ceremony of his new agency was a respectable event, attended by numerous dignitaries from the city.

In addition to his business endeavors, Ranjit continued to participate in adventurous motorcycle tours with his motorcycle group. A new highway, known as the Karakoram Highway, had recently been constructed, connecting the ancient Silk Route to China. This 1300 KM highway, which opened in 1978, linked the city of Kashgar in China's Xinjiang region to Abbottabad in Pakistan. The road mainly went through Pakistan occupied Kashmir in the Gilgit Baltistan region.

Ranjit and his group found this trip to be the most thrilling adventure back in 1978, so they decided to embark on the expedition during the summer. Ranjit's main goal for this journey was to gain more insight into the disputed region of Pakistan occupied Kashmir, also known as Azad Kashmir.

He also aimed to establish connections in the area, especially since many elites from Pakistan frequented

Azad Kashmir during the summer holidays, making it easier to approach them. Among these elites were the operatives of operation Gulfam, who had risen in ranks within the ISI.

The fourteen-day Karakoram journey proved to be both uneventful and enlightening for Ranjit. He discovered a lot about Azad Kashmir and how the Pakistani government enticed the locals to align with Pakistan. He also learned about the vacation spots of government officials, the luxuries they enjoyed, and the women who accompanied them during these trips.

The next person on the agenda was Rameez, who met his demise in Karachi.

Rameez

Rameez, in his mid-forties, had committed the killings of Sukhvinder and Ramesh two years ago. Sukhvinder met a swift death from a single bullet to the eye, while Ramesh suffered a gruesome fate with his dismemberment, gouged-out eyes, and eventual death from severe bleeding.

It was only fitting that Rameez's own demise would be painful and slow.

Ranjit, keeping a close watch on Rameez's movements through a contact, and was well aware of his habits. Rameez had a fondness for both liquor and women. Unlike many other places in Pakistan, obtaining liquor in

Karachi was relatively easier, with licensed shops and bootleggers supplying smuggled whiskey.

However, finding women was still a challenge. The main red-light district in Karachi, Napier Road, disguised its brothels as dancing halls and theaters due to the illegality of prostitution in Pakistan. The women referred to themselves as entertainers, performing mujra (dance), and arrangements for sexual services were typically made through private pimps. Rameez, funded by the ISI, often had women supplied to his hotel rooms by these pimps.

Ranjit had a trusted friend named Bilkis, an operative from the Baloch community.

Baluchistan, a troubled region in Pakistan, was home to the Balochis who faced exploitation by the Pakistani government.

Baluchistan was abundant in natural resources like petroleum, gas, oil, and minerals. Before the partition of India and Pakistan, the British granted independence to the Baluch Tribal councils, allowing them to impose their own taxes. So, when Pakistani forces attempted to gain access to Baluchistan after partition, the Baloch chiefs naturally resisted as the province had enjoyed independence and prosperity even during British rule.

Pakistan, driven by its desire for the region's resources, deemed the accession necessary. It took Pakistan around two years to coerce the Baloch leaders into accepting accession, which strained their relations.

Subsequently, there were three revolts in 1958, 1963, and 1972, all of which were brutally suppressed by Pakistan. The conflict eventually simmered down, but the scars remained.

The Pakistani government, however continued exploiting the natural resources, not doing much for the Baloch people. Basic necessities, such as clean water, access to education for children, have not been adequately provided by the Pakistani government.

Consequently, this lack of essential services caused greater frustration amongst Baloch, while lack of education caused their women to migrate to other parts of Pakistan working as dancers and prostitutes.

Bilkis was also one of the suppressed, working as a dancer in Karachi, but active as an operative. Through Bilkis, Ranjit got in contact with Riyaz, another operative, working as a pimp. Riyaz introduced Ranjit with a few working women, who could be of taste to Rameez.

One evening, when Rameez was having his drink at Hotel Marriot Karachi, Ranjit sat beside him at the bar, accompanying him were Farzana and Arzu, dressed in Black chiffon dresses, covering their sensual figures. While Ranjit continuously chatted with Farzana and Arzu, they both kept gazing at Rameez.

Ranjit left for the men's room; this is when Rameez made his move.

While Farzana smiled, Arzu seemed cautious that their husband would be back any movement. In the next few minutes, Rameez shared room number with Farzana and Arzu, should they both want to visit for some extra pleasure.

It was well past midnight when there was a knock on his door. Farzana and Arzu had come to visit after making sure their husband was tucked in bed. As they entered the room, they wasted no time undressing and asked Rameez if he wanted to have some real fun.

Rameez nodded in agreement, and Farzana proceeded to untie the bathrobe belt he was wearing, guiding him towards the bed.

They removed the belt from the bathrobe and used it to secure Rameez's hands and legs to the bed. They also used his socks to gag him, leaving the robe on his body with the front side exposed. With everything set, they opened the door for Ranjit.

Ranjit had brought along hydrochloric acid and a paintbrush. As Farzana and Arzu left the room, Ranjit began painting Rameez's front body with the acid. It was a slow and painful process that took over an hour, while Rameez screamed through the gag, unable to be heard.

When Ranjit finally dismembered him with a shaving blade, Rameez lost consciousness. Ranjit left the room, hanging the 'Do not disturb' sign on the doorknob.

Rameez was left in that state for another 48 hours, drifting in and out of consciousness. It wasn't until the hotel staff realized his reservation had expired that they used the master key to enter the room.

Rameez was rushed to the hospital, but his life couldn't be saved. His murder was investigated by ISI, but remained a mystery, as they could not find any clue.

Next on the list was Bakhtiar Kausar.

Bakhtiyar

Bakhtiyar, was an Army Captain in 1976, and had recently received a promotion to Major. He had killed Ashok and Sudesh, both of whom were killed with a single shot each.

Bakhtiyar was stationed at the Army Headquarters in Islamabad and was provided with an official Jeep. However, he preferred taking his wife out on a motorcycle. Every Sunday, they would ride his Honda motorbike together.

Their destination of choice was Shakarpariyan National Park on Murree Road, where they would spend two hours jogging and walking. Afterward, they would enjoy brunch at Hotel Ramada in the National Park before heading back to their official quarters in the cantonment.

To reach the park, Bakhtiyar would take Shaheed Sher Khan road to Islamabad highway, then turn right towards Srinagar Highway, and finally onto Murree road. The return journey followed the same route.

On one fateful day, a tragedy happened to Bakhtiyar and his wife. After brunch at Ramada, they were heading towards Murree Road when a speeding truck, unable to control itself on the narrow road, collided head-on with their bike.

The hotel staff promptly came to their aid, and they were rushed to the hospital. However, the impact of the accident had caused severe injuries, with one of Bakhtiyar's ribs piercing his heart, resulting in his instant demise. His wife, on the other hand, had to endure a two-month stay at the cantonment hospital before recovering as his widow.

Upon investigation, it was discovered that the truck had faulty brakes. The incident was deemed an accident, and the driver was released from jail after six months.

Following these tragic events, Imtiyaz, Mahboob, Anees, and Kasim became the next targets. The ISI became aware that the previous four deaths were not mere coincidences, prompting them to alert the remaining four members of Operation Gulfam.

Ranjit was informed, that after Gulfam, Imtiyaz and Anees were transferred to the Pakistan High Commission in London. Mahboob and Kasim were in Islamabad, but soon, mysteriously disappeared somewhere in Europe.

Ranjit stumbled upon the whereabouts of Mahboob and Kasim in January 1982. It was purely coincidental that he was able to find their trace. Surprisingly, through Mahboob, Ranjit also managed to discover the trace of Anees and Imtiyaz.

Mahboob and Kasim

They were distant relatives, both connected through their extended family. Kasim was the son of Mahboob's brother's sister-in-law. In 1978, they both had to leave Pakistan after receiving a warning from the ISI.

The mysterious deaths of four agents had raised suspicions, but it was unclear whether it was the work of a single rogue agent or the Indian agency. These deaths occurred in different provinces and in different ways, with the only common factor being the victims' involvement in the same operation. Despite the lack of connection, it was wise for the agents to remain cautious, to ensure their own safety.

During the late seventies and early eighties, Pakistan had begun supporting the Khalistan movement in various parts of the world, including India, Canada, and the UK.

Sikhs, known for their bravery, were specifically targeted by Pakistan to demand a separate Sikh state. The influence started in Toronto, Canada, where both Indians and Pakistanis coexisted peacefully. Harjyot Singh Mann, a Canadian resident who had migrated from Punjab, India, received support from the Pakistani ISI and declared himself as the President of Khalistan. This new state was intended to be carved out of Punjab, Haryana, and Himachal states in India.

Subsequently, ISI agents started visiting India from Canada and the UK, posing as guests of Indian Punjabis.

Pakistan pushed smuggled arms and ammunition from Pakistan and Canada to support the Khalistan cause.

On June 15th, 1981, Ranjit received his first lead on the whereabouts of Kasim and Mahboob. One of his contacts informed him that they had been disguising themselves as Sikhs and frequently traveling between Toronto, London, and Amritsar using fake documents.

In Punjab, Kasim went by the name Gurcharan Singh Virdi, a Sikh immigrant living in Toronto, who would visit his sick parents in Amritsar. Mahboob had taken on the identity of Sardar Jessa Singh, a self-proclaimed religious leader who had close ties with Harjyot Singh Mann.

Ranjit's contact also revealed that both Kasim and Mahboob were involved in inciting Sikh youths in Punjab to demand a separate Sikh state. They were under the protection of Mann's men, enjoying tight security.

From that point on, Ranjit instructed his contacts to closely monitor the activities of Kasim and Mahboob.

Since Mahboob had become a public figure, it would be easier to track his movements. On the other hand, keeping tabs on Kasim proved to be more challenging as he lived a more ordinary life.

The distance between Lahore and Amritsar was just a one-hour drive. Ranjit learned that Kasim was posing as the son of Nirmal Singh, who owned a flour mill and a shop in Atta Mandi, Amritsar. Nirmal Singh was a supporter of Harjyot Singh Mann and provided shelter to Kasim.

Ranjit decided to take advantage of the month of November in 1981, as many Pakistani Sikhs traveled to Amritsar during this time for the birthday celebrations of Guru Nanak Devji.

During this time, followers participate in 'Prabhat Pheris' every morning. These religious processions involve singing praises of Wahe Guruji in Punjab and other regions, through kirtan. The Pheris are held daily, starting a few weeks before Guru Nanak Dev Ji's birthday. This can be seen as a way for the community to prepare for the upcoming festival and connect with their religious beliefs. The procession typically begins at a central location and ends at a prominent Gurudwara or the home of one of the organizers.

Ranjit transformed his appearance to look like a Sikh, arranged his travel documents, and crossed the Attari border into Amritsar one beautiful morning by bus. The issue was that Ranjit didn't recognize Nirmal. He only had the address of Nirmal's Flour shop and mill.

On the first day, he went to the shop to purchase a 100 KG bag of flour. During the conversation, he mentioned to the shop assistant that the flour was intended for donation at the Golden Temple langar. He also inquired about a discount since he would be repeating this act for the next two weeks.

The assistant advised him to return in the evening when the shop owner, Sardar Nirmal Singh, would be present to discuss the discount.

In the evening, Ranjit returned to the shop and found Nirmal Singh waiting for him. Nirmal wasn't there to make a sale; he wanted to meet the 'Panthi' or religious man himself. Without hesitation, he offered a 'Dasses' or 10% discount, a gesture he had decided on long ago for Panthis.

Ranjit continued the conversation and informed Nirmal that he hailed from Lahore and had a strong desire to serve the Panth. He also mentioned that he actively participated in the Prabhat Pheris every day.

Impressed by Ranjit's dedication, Nirmal invited him to join the Prabhat Pheri in Dichau Kalan, which he had organized himself since his mill was located in that area.

The following day, Ranjit enthusiastically took part in the Dichau Kalan Prabhat Pheri and later visited Nirmal's home after the event concluded.

Over tea and snacks, Nirmal inquired about Ranjit's family in Lahore. Ranjit revealed that he had two sons and worked in the Maharaja Ranjit Singh Kitchen near Gurudwara Dera Sahib in Lahore. He mentioned that he would stay in Amritsar until Gurupurab and then return.

Since Ranjit had expressed his desire to serve the Panth earlier, Nirmal asked him about it.

Ranjit confirmed his commitment, prompting Nirmal to inform him that his son, Gurucharan, who resided in Toronto, would be visiting in January. Gurucharan had close ties with Sardar Jessa Singh, who was involved in running a Panth in both Amritsar and Toronto.

This news excited Ranjit as this was exactly what he had been waiting for. He continued to visit the shop and participate in the Prabhat Pheris until Gurupurab. On the day of Gurupurab, he bid farewell to Nirmal, promising to visit again in January.

True to his word, Ranjit returned to Amritsar on January 10th, 1982. He was introduced to Kasim as Gurucharan, by Nirmal Singh. This was the moment Ranjit had been eagerly waiting for. He immediately joined the Panth on the same day.

Ranjit explained to Gurucharan that initially, he would be visiting Amritsar intermittently due to his family in Lahore. However, he expressed his intention to eventually join full-time.

He understood that Gurucharan would take his time to introduce him to the leaders within the Panth, and until Gurucharan received a positive report from ISI, the secrets would not be shared. Ranjit was confident that ISI would provide positive feedback.

There was indeed one Ranjit Singh, employed in Maharaja Ranjit Singh Kitchen, who was a close associate of Ranjit. This particular Ranjit made sure to vanish whenever Ranjit was in Amritsar. The Kitchen had around 70 Sikh workers who were responsible for preparing the langar. Ranjit was confident that if anyone asked about him, the person in charge would simply refer to the workers' register to find his name. He also ensured that the photograph in the register was unrecognizable.

On March 29th, when Ranjit met Gurcharan again, Gurucharan happily introduced him to Sardar Jessa Singh. Jessa Singh had stationed himself inside the Golden Temple, where he preached to the youth every day, encouraging them to work for the Panth.

When Jessa was informed that Ranjit was willing to join the Panth, he sent him to the basement to meet with the other Panthis.

The halls in the basement were spacious enough to accommodate approximately 200 men and women. Many of them even stayed there overnight. Regular meetings took place and plans were made to establish Khalistan

Gradually, Ranjit discovered that those who stayed overnight were actually Pakistani Muslims pretending to be Sikhs. They were mostly ISI operatives who enticed Sikh youths, took them to Pakistan, trained them as terrorists, and then brought them back to fight against the Indian Government forces.

He was astonished to witness a continuous flow of beautiful young Sikh women who were enticed to serve the Panth, including offering their bodies to the Panthis. Overall, the entire setup had been orchestrated by the ISI, and now the Golden Temple was under their complete control.

After locating Kasim and Mahboob, Ranjit was determined to find trace of Anees and Imtiyaz before proceeding further. However, this task proved to be challenging as he had never seen either of them.

He was to be taken to Pakistan for initial training. He, being a resident of Pakistan, joined for training from Lahore itself. This training camp lasted for fifteen days, and training took place in Murree, which was in Pakistan occupied Kashmir.

Despite being a skilled operative, Ranjit had to conceal his capabilities and act like an ordinary person. Throughout the training, he sensed that the trainers were all ISI operatives.

To gather information, Ranjit discreetly placed recording devices in their barracks and individual rooms.

It took him approximately a month to obtain his first clue about Anees and Imtiyaz.

Interestingly, during the training, Mahboob had visited the training academy twice. He had a special chamber where he met the chosen individuals, and there was also a secret room within that chamber. While Ranjit managed to place a recording device in the chamber, he was unable to do so in the secret room.

Ranjit concentrated on the recordings from the chamber only. It was a seventeen-hour recording for both visits combined.

While during the daytime, the conversation was around the instructions being given to the trainers. During evenings and late hours, it was around casual talks.

Drinks and mutton biryanis were served during the evenings and Ranjit learned that Mahboob could not handle his drinks well.

It was difficult to understand his slurred talk, but during one of the discussions, Mahboob started boasting about his spoils during early days. It took some effort for Ranjit to understand, but soon enough Mahboob was talking about operation Gulfam of 1976.

He spoke about, how he killed Ravi and Rajendran. He also spoke about other kills by his associates. He spoke about Imtiyaz and Anees being his teammates and stated that they both were big men by now.

This was not enough information, but Ranjit was satisfied that Mahboob would lead him towards the last two operatives.

It was time for Mahboob and Kasim to bid farewell to the world. Not in Pakistan, but in India.

By June 1982, ISI sponsored terrorism started spreading in almost all of Punjab. By now, Ranjit became quite close to Mahboob and Kasim and accompanied them on their various tours of Punjab. He had amazing driving skills.

So, when he offered Mahboob to drive, Mahboob was impressed, and he immediately designated him as his driver.

Ranjit had to wait till December, when the winters arrived in Punjab. The days became short, there was fog during early mornings and evenings, which was what Ranjit was waiting for, to execute his plan.

During one trip from Malerkotla to Sangrur, Ranjit got his chance. Mahboob was alone in the car. Midway, Kasim was to be picked up from Dhuri. When Mahboob asked Ranjit to stop for a bio break, Ranjit prepared himself for some action.

He hit Mahboob on the head from behind. When he fell unconscious, he injected him with a sedative, to knock him out for a good time.

Ranjit loaded Mahboob in the car's trunk and took him to a nearby watch room in the fields, which usually remained unattended during this time of the year.

By October end, the fields are harvested, so these watch rooms are no longer needed till the next season. Before leaving him there, Ranjit injected another sedative, bound him tight, so Mahboob does not come out.

Now, he left to fetch Kasim.

Ranjit reached Dhuri and when he said that Mahboob was in the nearby fields, being served by the village head's wife, Kasim was not surprised.

Ranjit took Kasim too, to the same field, and when Kasim started walking in his front, Ranjit hit him too on the head.

Kasim was a bulky man. Lifting and shifting him to the watch room was not that easy, as in the case of Mahboob. Still, Ranjit managed.

He bound Kasim too and waited for them both to gain consciousness.

It was Kasim, who came to senses first.

Seeing him move, Ranjit shot him in the thigh. Kasim screamed frantically, which woke Mahboob. Next, Ranjit shot Mahboob in the thigh too.

When they both stopped screaming, Ranjit placed the proposal before them, to spill the whereabouts of Imtiyaz and Anees, if they wanted to live.

It took a further two shots, one on the other thigh and one on shoulder, when Kasim stated that Anees is third in line chief of ISI, stationed in Islamabad and Imtiyaz is a business tycoon, exporting textile and leather goods to Europe.

The moment Kasim shared the remaining details, there were two more gunshots, which eased Kasim and Mahboob out of this world.

Next day, Ranjit was back in Lahore, managing his bike distributorship.

Imtiyaz and Anees

It took almost four years, until Ranjit could finally get rid of Imtiyaz. Imtiyaz was an easy target, being a civilian. One of the laborers in his factory killed him in a failed robbery.

For Anees, Ranjit needed a thoroughly worked out plan. Anees being ISI chief, it seemed impossible to get him.

But so was for the Army General, who became Pakistan's President. So, they both went together. This was when Ranjit was already back in New Delhi.

One afternoon in September 1986, Mr. Naresh Khanna, the Indian Security Advisor received a phone call from a Pakistani number. The caller identified himself as Rameez, a used car salesman, who wanted to talk about a 1976 model Ford Mustang.

Naresh was happy to know about the car, which had gone missing in 1976.

It was agreed that Naresh would send someone to Kasur the next day around noon, where the car had gone missing and then would offer the price.

Kasur was a two-hour drive from Lahore. The car had disappeared from outside Al-Fayyaz Biryani center, so Ranjit arrived there on his motorbike at the agreed time and waited.

"Rameez miyan, Biryani Khilaoge?", a beautiful Baloch lady spoke to him, if he would order Biryani for her.

They ordered two Yakhni Pulao, which were finished by them while exchanging pleasantries. They got up, and Ranjit offered her to take to Ayub Falooda house, which the lady accepted.

In this area, Yakhni Pulao by Al-Fayyaz and Falooda by Ayub were famous. While they both finished their glasses of Falooda, still there was no talk about the real purpose.

Mahajabeen, as the lady was called, sat behind Ranjit on his motorbike and instructed to take her to Kings Hotel, on the outskirts of Kasur.

Mahajabeen knew her way in the hotel, as she was a working girl here. She had a permanent room booked for her special guests, to which she took Ranjit in.

They spent around two hours here. Mahajabeen asked for the Mustang and Ranjit told her that the car had been restored, after clearing all the earlier debts. This was an indication that all the persons involved in the killing of the 26 teammates, stand eliminated.

Now, Ranjit was ready for a bigger task.

Mahajabeen told him that someone would hand over travel documents and air tickets to Ranjit, for his travel to Dubai next week, on a family vacation. The family would stay in a leased apartment, specially chosen by the agency.

While Ranjit was leaving the hotel, the receptionist shared a knowing glance.

Mahajabeen stayed behind.

After reaching Lahore, Ranjit shared the good news with his wife Kubra, about the trip to Dubai. Due to frequent adventure trips of Ranjit, Kubra was habitual of handling the business on her own. As now, they both were traveling along with their sons, the showroom was decided to be closed for a week.

What made Kubra happier, that the trip was sponsored by Derbi motorcycles. It looked odd to Kubra, as she was aware of their sales achievements, but did not question more, as it was not frequent that the family was going on holiday together.

Dubai in those days was frequented just for shopping, as there were hardly any tourist attractions. They travelled to all the seven islands of UAE by road. A car along with the driver was in the sponsored package.

While the family was visiting the Al-Ain dairy, Ranjit saw Mahajabeen in another tourist group. While passing, Mahajabeen whispered to Ranjit to be at Delhi Darbar restaurant, sharp at 07:00 that night and to come alone.

Once back at the hotel, Ranjit informed Kubra that he had a meeting with representatives of Derbi, as they are launching a great sales scheme. Kubra wanted to tag along, but because of the boys, she had to remain in hotel.

At Delhi Darbar, Ranjit had to wait for some 20 minutes, and to his surprise, he saw Mr. Khanna walking towards him.

He was not expecting him, but one of his officers.

Mr. Khanna met Ranjit with great warmth. Although Ranjit was dead as far as the agency was concerned, but as his death was not confirmed, he was considered missing.

There were speculations within the agency that the person responsible for the deaths of all the killers of Quetta teammates, was the one who survived. Meeting with Ranjit confirmed this speculation for Mr. Khanna.

Ranjit wanted to know if he could start working again for the agency, as he missed that. He was aware that starting this line of work would require separation or complete isolation with his present family. But nation comes first. Besides, the king pin for the elimination of the team was still alive.

Mr. Khanna was thrilled. The morale at the agency was not what it used to be. Mr. Khanna could surely use agents like Ranjit. So, it was a 'yes', from him.

After returning from Dubai, Ranjit came back home with Mahajabeen one night. He introduced her to Kubra, as his new wife.

There was a fight, as anticipated. Kubra left home along with their sons that night.

She came back next morning with her parents and brothers.

Some more fist fights between the brothers and Ranjit. He was taken to hospital and then left there, with the instructions not to come back home.

Ranjit had not anticipated; this would end this easily.

Signing off all the property and showroom in favor of Kubra and his sons, Ranjit left Lahore the same night.

He stayed in the Royal hotel for a few days, then disappeared, only to be found in New Delhi a week later, with his original name and credentials.

During the next two years, the Pakistani president died in a plane crash, along with his close aides, while travelling from Dubai. The close aides included Anees Bari, the chief of ISI.

There was a technical snag in his plane, which the Dubai authorities failed to detect.

The plane crashed near Multan, but the more disgraceful news was, the presence of very large amount of money and property documents, in the plane, which the Pakistani government or the president's family could never explain.

The president, who was the Army general, had dethroned the earlier prime minister of the country and within three years, hanged him publicly. During his reign, the president kept declaring himself as an honest man. But the discovery of ill-gotten wealth, post his death, could never be explained.

By January 1987, Ranjit was back in India for good.

He worked with the agency for another twenty years, during which he was instrumental in controlling Punjab

Terrorism, the disputed structure in Ayodhya and riots thereafter. He slowly rose to seniority in the agency and by 2007, he was the chief. He was twice given an extension in service, and finally he retired from the agency in 2012. Even after retirement, he remained associated in the country's security advisory committee.

There was a change of Government in India in 2014, starting a period known as Golden Phase of India.

The new prime minister recalled Ranjit from retirement and appointed him as National Security advisor.

Ranjit proposed a comprehensive plan, known as *Operation Brihadratha*, to the new prime minister. This plan aimed to strengthen India's borders and defense system while also focusing on enhancing the road infrastructure. The ultimate goal was to ensure the long-term security of the Indian borders by integrating infrastructure development into the operation.

During the same time, Ralph Stevens, the chief of CIA met with Ranjit, as the CIA had a similar project, which they called *Project Wall*.

Ralph had already identified Prince for the project. Ranjit knew, Prince could be a pain, still went ahead and approved his name.

By the end of 2017, Ranjit found the approach of CIA not meeting with the Indian desire, being USA centric and extremely violent. India henceforth distanced itself from Project Wall.

Now The Prince was responsible solely for *Brihadratha*. *Project Wall* was directly supervised by Ralph's team, headed by the Brit, Jon Russel. Jon was actually chosen by Prince for *Brihadratha* but did not mind his shifting to *Project Wall*.

CHAPTER 14

Jon Russel

August 2016. Prince had a meeting with Jon Russell for lunch during the first week. As Prince had met me before the meeting, he took me along for introductions.

Jon was the Police Captain with London Metro Police and was quite a decorated officer. He was the one, who had solved the 2011 London bombing case, wherein scores of Londoners were killed and property worth millions was destroyed. Jon and his team had cracked the case within three days, and all accused were given the electric chair, the following year.

He was quite a celebrity in London. Apart from the London bombings, he had solved many other serious crimes within days. Incidentally, as he resided on Baker Street, London, and due to his quick solving of crimes, he was known as modern day Sherlock Holmes.

Many believed he was really close to some very influential ministers, and that was the cause of his quick promotions. These types of stories are spread for all those whose career graph rise is early.

Jon was taking retirement from Police job soon, and this meeting was for the purpose of his future employment. There was no growth left for him. Although he was promised a political post, he wanted to continue doing something exciting. Prince had exactly the same to offer him, hence, this meeting.

The restaurant was nothing fancy. We had chosen 'Nandos' in Piccadilly, Central London.

This was an early lunch meeting, as we had to discuss it at length. Jon was at Nandos, exactly at noon. So were Prince and me. The manager of the restaurant recognized Jon, so there was no trouble choosing our seats. We chose a corner table. While The Prince hugged Jon, I shook hands with him.

Prince had known Jon for ages. While Prince worked with the agency, he had come in contact with Jon many times. Jon was a bulky man. Six foot plus, 250 pounds, round clean-shaven face, and head, with a dash of silver-gray stubble.

Before meeting Jon, Prince had shared his history and also about London, which most people did not know. Prince told me about Jon and his ways of solving crimes quickly. Jon's success thrived on the illegal migrant population of London. "while citizens have rights, illegal migrants have none. All cops have to do is put the blame on them, supported by some placed evidence, and just deport them. Even if you put them in jail or they are awarded capital punishment, there is no outcry."

Prince further told me about the illegal population of UK, he said, 'Yes, the government knows about them. In fact, they are a boon for the UK economy'. As I seemed puzzled, he explained,

'You see, the British have been the rulers of the world, and don't like to work. It is below their dignity, being the rulers.

So, earlier, whenever they were leaving a country, they asked for volunteers to migrate to the UK. These migrants worked as house helps. Their children educated in UK, still had the dedication of their migrant parents, so worked hard.'

'After some time, the UK encouraged the illegal migrants. The legally migrated people were sent home once in a while, where they praised life in the UK. This prompted many people to come to the UK. Many came legally, but a large chunk was of illegal migrants. The government exactly knows, how many of these illegals have come to UK and where they have settled.'

He continued, 'as I said earlier, UK population does not like to work. The socio economy structure is designed in such a way that if you work for 15 years and have paid taxes during that time, you are entitled to a lifelong fixed pension and your medical bills are on government'.

'So, the Brits complete these 15 years, and almost 40% of these, are later a burden on UK's the exchequer. While working too, they have fixed hours, holidays, family time and so many other perks.'

'But these illegal migrants, who work full time, without a break and being illegal, are not entitled to full wages. So, most of the construction contractors, shops, malls, cab operators, factories, cleaning companies, employ these illegal migrants. They have no official records, hence at the time of any casualty, they are off the compensation list. This helps building the UK."

With this above chat, I wondered, had anything changed? The only change I could see was, earlier, the Brits exploited other countries by invading them and staying in those countries. Now, they exploited the same people, by inviting them to migrate to UK, work for them at lower cost, contribute to the UK's economy, still having no rights of their own.

It was again these people, who, having migrated from the Villages of the third world, facilitated the food and dairy exports from their respective countries. Ensured the UK gets the best products at cheaper rates.

During this lunch meeting, Prince took the first half hour to explain, what was expected out of Jon.

Jon was retiring soon. He had an incomparable depth of knowledge about legal and illegal migration population in the UK. So, Prince wanted Jon to select Asian migrants, train them and provide them to help in Project Wall. These migrants would provide information about their countries, and later, were to be sent to their home countries, for specific purposes, which Prince would share later. I was introduced as the contact point for this project.

It was decided that Jon would keep connecting me with the desired people and also provide me the inside information about activities of South Asian migrants.

Jon would also train some people for me, for which there would be separate contracts between Jon's new company and another security company. This company was to be registered in the UK but worked as a front for me.

Jon officially retired in March of 2017 and in June, he joined MI8 academy solely to train agents for Project Wall. The trainees included Yang, which till then I did not know. Apart from Yang, there was this Pakistani couple, Faridah, and Ismail, a few Tibetans, Vietnamese, and Sri Lankans. These trainees were to help later in Project Wall or Brihadratha.

Jon also started connecting me with a few immigrants, who were from Pakistan occupied Kashmir (POK). In exchange of sponsorship for their permanent residency, these immigrants provided me with the information about the exact locations of terrorist training camps in POK.

I passed on the information about these locations to the Indian Government through coded messages. This helped the successful operation of surgical strike at POK.

At least seven terrorist camps were destroyed by India Air Force.

By now, there was enough hysteria against Pakistani terrorism. When the Pakistani representative raised the surgical strike issue in the UN, no one paid any heed. A great coordinated effort by government of India.

In December, Jon took me to a wedding in South Hall, London. The wedding was of a Pakistani migrant couple, who were part of Project Wall. They were known as Faridah and Ismail. Jon wanted to introduce me to some people, who could help me further on the mission.

Here is, when I met a young lady, who resembled Yang.

She looked different, not only because of her figure, but the face was also different. It was only when I read recognition in her eyes, I was sure of her to be Yang.

What was she doing in London? Was she married?

I sure was going to find out. But before I could contact her, she went with the bride in the ladies' section of the celebration. This being a Muslim wedding, men were not allowed in the ladies' section.

In January 2018, I received a message from Jon to meet him in St. James club at Pall Mall.

This was the club for the elite and entry was not permitted if one was not accompanied by a member. When Jon took me inside, it was obvious that he was a member and the money provided by us was doing good for him.

At his table, there was a tall, slim brunette, who looked like a model in her mid-twenties. Knowing Jon, it was for sure, she was not his daughter or any other relative. Her mannerism also reflected; she was none.

It amused the beauty when my gaze lingered a few moments longer than required. Obviously, she had some silicon in her body to give it shape, which invited men.

I was offered a drink, which I took in order to stretch the meeting. I wanted another, when the first finished. I was still analyzing the girl, when Jon interrupted and stated, "have any number of drinks, but before that, let's talk about the issue we were meeting for". How rude.

Jon was supposed to share with me some lists of individuals, which I had asked him to provide. Jon's team had prepared the list for me, which Jon shared. As I wanted to discuss the list, Jon cut me short by saying, he and Elina (the girl's name) are going to his room. I may read the list and then if I needed anything further, I could come to his office in the morning.

"And by the way, please settle the bill on your way out. This is table 26".

'Son of a Bi$#&%'.

But this is what this information cost.

The bigger surprise for me was when I saw the bill. The service charges were mentioned as £1,000. I felt like a jackass, as it was Jon who was enjoying Elina's service, and I was paying the bill.

I went home. Poured myself a drink. I had to read the entire list, prepare a summary, then code it and send it to New Delhi. Having nothing else to do, I started on the same.

An hour later, my doorbell rang.

I was not very surprised to see Elina or how she got my address. I had left a good tip for her along with my address, while settling the bill.

She already knew she was paid by me. As Jon had finished fast and went home to his wife, she found it interesting to spend the night with me.

What the heck, it was already midnight in New Delhi. The report can be sent in the morning, before the office opens.

She asked for the bathroom, left the door open while she showered. After a few minutes, I helped her clean herself.

She went home in the morning. Although there was no deadline to submit the report, I started working on it immediately.

Jon's team had done good work. The list contained the names and contact details including phone numbers, of students, sponsored by China and other countries, and who had some relation with bureaucracy.

Soon, I started using the list. There were messages sent on their phones, which started installing bugs on the phones of these unsuspecting students.

For the time being, the bugs were just relaying the recordings, at a facility at some undisclosed location in East India.

By this time, Indian Government separated themselves from Project Wall. Project Wall was now supervised by Jon full-time. Prince and I moved to Project Brihadratha.

During December 2019, Prince came to his ancestral Estate in Eddington. One evening he invited me to the estate through a coded message.

I reached the estate and found Prince in the Tennis court. He was in the middle of the game. The opponent was a girl, much younger than him.

When the game broke, Prince and the girl came to where I was sitting. When the girl removed the cap, I could see some familiarity. This was the same girl; I had seen in the Muslim wedding.

"You both must be knowing each other. From now on, you both would work together"

So, this was Yang. What was she doing here? What had she done to her face? Moreover, how did Prince know that we knew each other? Yang and I had met briefly in New Delhi. Is there anything which is hidden from this man?

From the tennis court, we left towards the main building. Prince and Yang were sweating even in this December winters. They both went to take quick showers while I was asked to pour myself a drink. They were back in some twenty odd minutes, looking fresh in changed clothes.

Prince poured himself a drink and one for Yang. During casual conversation, he told us that soon we would be initiating another project. Yang had a list of children of some Chinese bureaucrats, who are getting their education in London. They, along with the ones on my list, were to be used for project Brihadratha.

Brihadratha meant financial doom for China, so it no longer is able to support Tibet. These children of bureaucrats would help us achieve this fate. They would provide us China's business plans, as well as details of investments with bank details.

Thereafter, we enjoyed our drinks, then dinner and soon it was time for bed for Prince. He had a fixed bedtime at 10:00 PM.

While Yang was having a post dinner stroll, I approached. "Never knew a beauty like you could be working for something like this".

Yang smiled and said, "never knew I would be meeting the rich spoilt brat like you, in these circumstances."

"We can catch up on some conversation during the night", I said.

It was a cold December night. Soon we ended our walk and settled down in the library.

We started chatting. I was surprised to know that Yang was already working similar projects, when I met her first in 2009. So, she had been a senior to me by at least six years.

It made sense now, why she had rejected my friendship. Finally, it was a relief that it had nothing to do with me. Yang had 'Free Tibet' in mind even in those days. And now, it was her destiny.

When I told her about me, she was unmoved with my sharing about my parents' untimely accidental death. Her parents were also killed (she used the word killed) when she escaped to India from Dadong.

As we discussed further, I shared the worst thought which kept haunting me for a long time. The possibility that the accidental death of my parents could have been created for securing my work at the agency.

Yang was unperturbed and continued, "I have seen this happening before, this happens all the time in our type of work". Her advice was, "the best way is to move on with it, as now there is no return and nothing will change, except for you finding yourself in a cremation ground".

During January 2020, a chance discussion in India house with a visitor from New Delhi, confirmed my thoughts.

There was an attractive visiting guest from New Delhi, whom I met at India House Café. She was in London in connection with some official work.

It was a Thursday, and the café served 'Kheema Pav'.

While we were enjoying that on the shared table, we started chatting.

This lady guest had a deathly gaze, which could make anyone shiver with fear. Her name was Anita, or that was what she told me. She was from New Delhi, so we clicked instantly. I introduced myself as the Personal Security officer to the finance attaché.

While her gaze could make anyone uncomfortable, her body was inviting, perhaps due to extreme workouts.

The finance attaché had meetings the entire day at India House. Anita had nothing to do that day, so we continued to chat beyond teatime.

By 5:00, the finance attaché was to leave for home, so I got up. She did not have any plans for dinner, so I asked if she wanted some Indian food.

When she said yes, I invited her home.

I dropped the attaché to his home, then left for mine.

It was snowing in London and the temperature was − 10°C. Christmas was over, still the shops, commercial establishments, and apartments all were decorated with lights.

Anita rang my doorbell sharp at 7:30 PM. It had started to get dark, and the lights were on. The moment I opened the door, she entered the cozy room to avoid the chill.

While inside, she removed her coat, providing another glimpse of an inviting figure. Even while fully clothed, the hugging dress she wore provided a full shape of what was underneath.

We sat on the couch, enjoying our first drink. While I was having Famous Grouse, she chose to have Gin. I had Monkey 47 which I poured generously.

Being already in London for over three years now, I had shifted from official quarters and had taken an apartment in Bethnal Green, Central London. The area was majorly inhabited by seasoned Indian community, so I could feel at home here.

There were many home chefs available, from whom I could get home made Indian food.

Today I called Pummy auntie, a Sikh lady, who cooked awesome mutton. So, it was mutton Rogan josh and roti for today, with some rice and dal.

Pummy auntie drove a Vauxhall Corsa and she made the deliveries herself. By the time our dinner arrived, we were already finishing our third drink.

Dinner was piping hot. So, while Anita poured our fourth drink, I started setting the table. I could tell Anita was enjoining every moment being here. She was in a light mood and the stern gaze was nowhere to be seen.

Just out of nowhere, I asked her body count. She knew instantly, I was not asking about her bed partners, but how many she had killed.

There was a small pause and the deathly gaze returned. "How do you know" she asked.

"Well, I am not a kid or fool, I have undergone training". I continued, "you can skip replying to this, just enjoy the best meal you can get, while in London".

We did not speak after that, till I served her Pummy auntie's specialty, Gulab Jamuns. They were already cold, so I had to heat them in Microwave for a few seconds.

When she took her first bite, I could sense she liked them.

Then she spoke. "I have killed many, perhaps more than a hundred, as I have lost count."

We both knew she was not supposed to share this with anyone, and I don't know why she did, but she continued.

"You see, my job is to get the hurdles cleared from the path of the agency." She took a pause then continued,

"Then there are many incidents, which are considered natural calamities, disasters or acts of God, in fact many of them are staged to either get rid of a particular group of people or community or a government."

"Also, the Agency on many occasions comes with a situation wherein they have identified a perfect asset, but there is something or someone which does not allow the chosen one to join our work. This is where I come in handy. We have to stage some sort of an accident, so while the asset does not know what happened, we get our asset's full dedication".

The same deathly gaze, which I had seen in the morning, returned for a while. It conveyed to me what she meant.

I re-lived the night of February 14-15, 2016. I started getting uncomfortable with the thought of what could have happened with my parents. I kept my cool and progressed calmly to know more.

She had finished her Gulab Jamun, got up, placed the bowl in the dish washer.

It was already 10:30 PM and had started to snow again. I offered her, if she wanted to stay, I could arrange a foldable bed.

This time, it was she, who said with a smile, "we are no kids. I can sleep on your bed. Moreover, I know from your gaze since morning what you want."

I was not my usual self during the entire episode of love making. The question kept haunting me, "was my parents' accident a staged act and was it her"?

Having no other way of finding, I asked her while she was wearing her skirt. "Were you on a mission in Delhi during February 2016"?

"I don't recollect", she said while she momentarily froze.

It was this momentary shocked expression on her face, which gave me the reply.

She did not have to answer or lie like this. I did not want the answer anymore. I had got one.

It was still snowing, but she called for a cab and left for her hotel.

I did not sleep that night. At that moment, I despised the agency, Anita and people like her.

So, my destiny was designed by the agency? I kept contemplating, should I continue or quit.

Quitting meant nothing for the agency but would make my life miserable. I would have to live under constant threat, as Anita would certainly report the last conversation with her, when she was back in New Delhi.

Also, if I quit, there would be no chance, I'll ever get to know the whole truth and would never be able to avenge the deaths of my parents.

Even if I continue, this conversation shared by her would put me constantly under the radar. I should not have asked the question. It was a mistake, but it was late by now. I had to think fast, as she was in London for another day or two.

Next two days, there was no untoward incident reported in the news, while she stayed. But there was an accident on London – Bath highway, causing loss of life for a migrant couple, who had no identification on them. The man was driving at 90 miles per hour speed, when somehow, he lost control of the car. The car hit the road divider at high speed. The pieces of the car and the bodies within had to be scooped up, piece by piece by the highway authorities.

CHAPTER

Forming the Team

After passing from MI8 academy, Yang shifted to a small apartment in Brick Lane, Central London. This apartment, she was to share with three others, Ismail, Faridah, and Lasith. While Ismail and Faridah were from Pakistan and about to be married, Lasith was from Sri Lanka.

Ismail and Faridah were first cousins. While Faridah was born in London, Ismail had joined her last year. Ismail had come to London under political asylum scheme.

This scheme was often misused by third world countries, especially from disturbed Muslims countries. They only had to make an application to the British High commission in their respective countries, claiming that they belonged to a disturb area and there is threat to their life. The British High commission desired some affidavits and other confirmations from the local authorities, which were procured at a cost, through corrupt means, by the applicant. Once that done, British government issued a provisional Visa to the applicant, to stay in UK. Once these applicants visited the UK, they never left. In

Ismail's case, he was to be later used for Project Wall, hence there were further concessions.

Faridah's parents stayed in South Hall. She had four sisters and two brothers. Her father ran a video library. He had moved to United Kingdom, at the age of 26 again, under political asylum scheme.

In Faridah's own words, her father was deported some four times, but every time he came back, one way or the other. As for Faridah's mother and all the children, they were born in the UK, hence they were natural citizens. Ismail was son of Faridah's uncle. The uncle, who was the brother of Faridah's father, stayed back in Peshawar.

Lasith was on government scholarship, from Sri Lankan Government. His father was part of the Sri Lankan army, which was supported by Indian Government during late 1980s, uprooting the Tamil liberation movement and was martyred during one of the operations. Cost for his travel, studies, boarding, and lodging was taken care by Sri Lankan government.

It was normally believed that various governments across the developing countries and China, funded the foreign education for their extremely studious students, in major universities in developed countries. The given cause for the same, was to encourage the deserving talent.

However, the actual reason for this was, the students were expected to pass with flying colors, secure jobs in these countries. And once that was done, over the period become citizens, rise to the decision-making authority in respective companies or Government agencies, with the sole aim to benefit the business of the sponsoring countries.

Yes, this was a long bet, these countries took, but it ultimately benefitted the growth of their business abroad. Till then, the families of these students were closely tracked, one wrong move by students, and the parents were answerable.

The Governments knew that Sri Lankan, Chinese and other third-world countries promoted deeper family values, and the children cared for their parents' wellbeing, much like the parents did, for them. Hence, they remained compliant with the wishes of the governments.

There were two things common amongst these four students. They all were extremely sharp, agile, and studious, and they all were highly trained in un-armed combat. They were all a part of Project Wall.

The entire Brick Lane area was considered to be occupied by Asians, mainly people from Bangladesh and China. Although, the area comes under Zone-1 or Central London, but the property cost and rents were low here, as English or Europeans did not want to stay here.

In the mid-19th century, this area was considered to be highly unsafe. Occupied by many bars and pubs, wherein Navy and Merchant Navy sailors drank and womanized. Robbery, violence, and alcohol dependency were commonplace, and the endemic poverty drove many women to prostitution to survive.

Not only this, but poverty also drove many men to petty offences, even bigger crimes like robbery and killings. During this time, not very far from here, lived the infamous serial killer, who was named 'Jack the Ripper' by media, as he affected countless murders. This serial killer, who was never caught by the police, used to target the prostitutes. He used to rob them, kill them with sharp weapons and later mutilated their private parts.

Things improved in the 20th and early 21st century, and yet this area was not considered habitable by the British.

There were three storied row houses with a basement, sharing a common wall with each other. The houses were owned by migrated Asians, or were leased to the students, migrants or to people working odd jobs. As Bangladeshis and Pakistanis kept on increasing their numbers, many mosques started appearing, in place of the churches.

The apartment, where Ismail, Yang, Faridah, and Lasith stayed, was also in one such apartment complex, named Merlin apartments, which was developed after demolishing the Commercial Street Church.

This was a three-room apartment, on the second floor of the building. Basement, ground and first floor were rented out to other students, mainly from China. Hence, was the reason why this was chosen for Project Wall.

Yang, because of her Mongolian looks was often taken as a Chinese. She could also speak different dialects in Mandarin. Soon, she made friends with a group of Chinese students. She was now seen as a part of Chinese groups, as she hung out with them often.

She selected a few students, whose parents were high ranking Chinese government officials, she started spending much time with them. These students were engineering graduates from China, pursuing master's in advanced cyber security from Lords university, London.

By end of February 2018, while the entire London was covered in white snow, suddenly these Chinese students group received a dictate, that their scholarships were cut down by the government. Soon, some officials from Chinese embassy barged into their rooms, taking away all their belongings, leaving them high and dry. Yang was much supportive to this group and came to their rescue.

She was earning a good side salary and tips by working in a pub and she offered to pay the group's rent, till they found an alternate means to pay. Fortunately, their Student Visa was provided by UK government, hence the officials from Chinese embassy could do nothing to impound that.

Now, Yang was the closest to an angel, as far as this Chinese group of students were concerned. They never realized that the reason for their withdrawing of support by Chinese government, was none other but Yang.

These students were now a steady source of confidential information from China.

It was the new year's party in 2017. The students had organized a bash at the college gym to welcome 2018. The booze was flowing, music was loud, and everyone danced like there was 'no tomorrow'.

By around midnight, everyone in a drunken state started removing their clothes. Few, including Yang started clicking pictures on their mobile phones.

Next morning, while Yang shared those pictures with her Chinese friends, she secretly passed on a bug through her phone, which the Chinese mobiles could not detect.

The bug first erased its source of entry and later scanned the entire information on the targeted phones.

Within days, the bug mutated. When these Chinese students shared some information with their parents, it transferred to their parents' phones. This chain continued, and by mid-January, all the communications between different Chinese authorities, started reaching an undisclosed destination.

The raid by the Chinese Embassy officials was, as the authorities in China had identified a breach. But as the seized equipment from the students revealed no such trace, they were pardoned, and their scholarships resumed.

This new group of Yang consisted of three girls and two boys. There was Pauline, Tricia, Grace and then Alex and Joe. They all had added Christian names to their Chinese ones, for ease of pronunciation by Brits.

After the initial support offered by Yang for initial few days, they all took part time jobs in different businesses within London to support themselves. This was an added income they started, should there be a change of mind by Chinese government. Thankfully, the year was 2018, and the job scenario was still good in the UK.

By April, this group was called to the Dean's office, where a final blow awaited them. There were officials from Chinese Embassy, who wanted to take the group with them. The Dean had no choice but to hand them over, as the Embassy officials were accompanied by Metro Police.

Once inside the Chinese Embassy, the freedom the UK offered, was gone, as it was Chinese territory. The law of the respective country is applicable inside the four walls of the Embassy.

The five were stripped, their entire body was X-rayed for any hidden chips. After that, they were wired for lie detection and grilled continuously for four hours, simultaneously, in separate rooms.

Apparently, the Chinese government met a dead end with their investigations.

Their investigation had started in January, when during a routine check, a few of the phones of Chinese officials were found with a trace of an unidentified bug. Thereafter, they investigated a large group of people in China, whose phones were identified to be hacked. By tracing the links, the investigators could find a common link, the parents of these five students.

Thankfully, this group of five was not as sharp. They could never link their miseries to Yang. When they were questioned by the authorities if there was any sharing of files over phone, there was an awfully long list of students who shared photos and texts with them. So, Yang was not pin pointed.

After their interrogation, they could not be detained any further, as UK and Metro Police were already aware about their capture. They were Chinese citizens, but on UK soil.

So, there were two choices for the Embassy staff. Either to take them back to China or set them free in UK. The staffers could never take the risk of taking them back to China, as they were exposed to risk. So, they were made to sign an agreement, wherein the five surrendered their rights of liberty before Chinese authorities and later accepted an unconditional exile from China.

On the hindsight, they would have been happy for the exile. The only pain was the separation from their loved ones.

By July, their studies were complete. They had to wait another month for the results. Yang had become really close with this group and almost every day, they had a sleepover at one's place or the others.

The dark period for the Chinese group was almost over by now. They all had appeared for campus placements. While Pauline, Tricia and Grace were selected by British Banks to work in their Cyber security teams, Alex and Joe were selected by an Indian multinational IT company, which offered cyber security expertise to various European and American banks.

By September 11, 2018, the Chinese group joined their respective companies. The Chinese group continued to stay together for some more time. Now they were earning good. By June 2019, they all shifted to their respective individual flats, within London.

The group was under much gratitude, for what Yang had done for them, could not think of losing her friendship. On weekends, they all would keep meeting. She would get firsthand information on Chinese policies through this group. Yang could know the latest developments with Chinese government. She kept sharing a bug on a routine basis, which provided a continuous stream of information. The new bugs were advanced. They kept destroying the trace, when they approached another phone.

Alex amongst the group was more adventurous and would keep exploring different things in Cyber security. By August 2019, he had developed some tool, which could penetrate any system with weak security and provide a synopsis of the data available in that system.

When Yang asked, he confirmed that the tool could detect various access-controlled files and, it could pass the firewalls. The tool could also detect the accessibility of each user in the system, including the administrator, and could take over the role of the administrator.

This was huge for Yang. The development reminded her of Ming. She wanted to pass on her plan to The Prince.

This is what she did, before the tennis game at his Estate, in December of 2019.

By now, Project Wall was already split. While Jon Russel was managing Project Wall with the assistance of Faridah, Ismail and Lasith, Prince was in-charge of Project Brihadratha with Yang and Adwait.

CHAPTER 16

The Revenge

During December 2019, Anita was tasked to get rid of Hameed Husain, the Pakistani double agent, who was running a terrorist camp, near India-Pak border. He was responsible for the multiple attacks on Indian forces, during 2014 to 2016 and after the Indian surgical strike, again was planning something big to take revenge. He was in the UK for employing some hitmen. He had to be stopped.

Anita went missing. Even by January end, Anita had not filed her report. In fact, she had not reported for duty, either at India house London, or in New Delhi.

The night before, she was seen with me.

In a casual conversation, I was asked by another security staff at India House, if she had disclosed any plans before her disappearance. I knew nothing, is what I stated.

She was in my home till, a little later than dinner. I was sure the agency guys knew how much longer she was at my place, so without asking I said that we shared the bed, post which she left. There was no need to talk about the conversation we had.

In any case, I was sure the agency would by now, know that she stayed at her Hotel that night. She was to be picked up by one of her friends the next morning. The agency would have gone through the CCTV footage by now. I was in India House throughout that day. So, I was covered from being a suspect.

I knew the agency would wait for another week, before declaring Anita AWOL. Post that, there would be limited enquiries, as the agency had a history of agents becoming rogue.

What I did not share was, after the fourth drink, Anita had told me that she planned to take Hamid to Bath in his car and quietly cause a 'chemically induced heart attack', while he was having fun with her.

Anita had met Hamid at the weekly auction at Hilton hotel, Kensington. To start the conversation, she complimented Hameed on his winning bid on the year 1896 Samurai sword. Hameed was attentive when Anita talked about the history of the sword.

She then causally mentioned a collection of her own swords in her residence in Bath.

"I would surely be interested, my dear lady, to have a look at the swords, and a Bath", Hameed quipped suggestively. He offered her a drink at the Avenue Bar, which Anita accepted.

Anita had introduced herself as widow of an erstwhile Lord. Her accent and gate matched the description. The conversation continued for a couple of drinks and by dinnertime, Hameed again showed interest in her collection of swords.

Anita smiled and asked him to pick her up at 07:00 Saturday morning from Piccadilly.

Bath was 115 miles from London and was famous for ancient Roman Baths. Anita had arranged a river-facing mansion near Clevedon Harbor, which she had planned to display as her own. The mansion had a history and was owned by one of the ancient families. The ancient family had lost their fortune and now offered the mansion for rent. The decor inside the mansion had numerous collectibles to display.

It was unfortunate that they could not reach Clevedon. Midway, the car's windscreen caught a wandering rock.

The rock first hit the windscreen, then Hameed at such high speed, who lost consciousness instantly. The car wavered, hit the road divider, and went flying to the other side of the highway. This happened at such speed that neither Hamid nor Anita could gain control of the vehicle. They both died instantly.

The highway authorities, who reached the accident spot, had a difficult time collecting all the pieces of the two bodies and matching them.

The car was a rental, rented on a fake ID. The bodies had no identification on them. So, the authorities stored the bodies in the public morgue for a week, then buried them. They, being declared as immigrants without documentation, there was no probe, any further.

Agency knew that Anita was to execute Hameed. How? She had not shared.

Now, there was no trace of Hameed and Anita also had gone missing. So, the agency waited for Anita for a month, and then declared her AWOL. Another agent was deputed to trace and execute Hameed.

Next day, after the accident, I received a call from Raunak Jayasinghe, who wanted compensation for the rock. I promised he would receive the same at his home by the next day.

Jayasinghe was working as a cab driver with Hertz rent-a-car. He was already involved in the double murder of his agent, who had facilitated his migration to the UK and his girlfriend, whom he had caught having fun with the agent.

He was already pissed off with the two. His agent could not complete his documentation even after three years. On the other hand, his girlfriend whom he had to marry for permanent residency, was avoiding the question of marriage.

Having found them sleeping in his bed and in his home, was reason enough for Jayasinghe to shorten the two lives.

He pulled the butcher's knife from the kitchen without noise. The agent was in deep sleep, so first he stabbed the girl on neck, she died instantly.

Then he moved toward the agent. The agent took some time to die, as the stab missed the trachea (windpipe) and Jayasinghe had to overpower the agent for the second stab. Still the agent tried to escape, creating a mess of blood in the entire room.

Sadly, now Jayasinghe would have to clean the mess even more.

Jayasinghe wrapped the bodies in sheets, placed them in his cab and carefully cleaned the entire house for any blood stains. Then he drove the cab to the outskirts of London to dispose of the bodies in a ditch.

What Jayasinghe did not realize was that the agent had a wife. She was not able to contact him for two days and reported to the police officers.

The police officers traced the location of phone calls made and received from the phone of the agent to draw a pattern. The last call was received in the same area where Jayasinghe lived.

The street had CCTV coverage. One of the cameras had captured the faint image of Jayasinghe, struggling to put two large packages in his cab, late at night, then driving off.

No explanations were convincing enough for the police officers, who saw something amiss.

He was caught. His cab's GPS gave the location for that night.

The bodies were recovered, chemical examination of his home matched the blood type and here was a fool proof case.

Jayasinghe, being an illegal migrant, did not have any rights in the UK. He was to be given the electric chair.

He was the perfect one, I could use for any operation now. So, I arranged for his bail through Jon. I also promised an English bride for him for permanent residency.

For Project Anita, he only had to travel mid-way to Bath, hide behind a tree and throw a rock at the right time. For this, he was paid ten thousand pounds.

By mid-March of 2020, I was still contemplating whether to be with the agency or leave. The realization of how I was orphaned was too much to bear. This is when COVID19 started, and the countries faced lockdowns.

The disease started causing a large number of deaths in various parts of the world. In London too, the lockdown was imposed, and life came to a standstill.

While I had the option to remain in India House, at least my daily needs could have been looked after. I preferred to stay at home and contemplate my life ahead. Post Anita episode, I presumed that it was Prince, who had ordered the killings of my parents. But I was still not sure.

At present, the world was at stand still. So was I. locked myself in my home in Bethnal Green. Pummy auntie proved to be the mother I had lost. She made sure I was fed well during the entire four months of lockdown.

By July 2020, the world travel started.

Last four months, I kept thinking. I had already lost my parents, which now I realized was due to the agency. If I leave the agency now, I would never be at ease. Also, if I join my brother and his family in business, I might invite trouble for them as well.

The loss of my parents could never be compensated, even if I kill Prince.

On the other hand, now, as I was working for my country, I could do wider good. It was not that it was only me who could have done that. But I had already started in that direction. So might as well finish.

I took two decisions. One, to sever all connections with my brother and his family for their own security. Two, work with double zest to pay homage to my parents' sacrifice.

There was a third decision, never to disclose anything about my knowledge on my parents' death, with anyone and if Prince was the one calling the shots for that, a revenge fit to pay homage to my parents should follow.

I never discussed Anita with anyone till date. But I made a quick travel to New Delhi, just to know some facts.

I needed some answers, and I was not doing anything further till I get them. So, on July 30, 2020, I travelled to New Delhi, went straight to the building where I had met Prince for the first time.

On reaching there, I did not find the bulky man or the sexy beauty, who had received me earlier. I could enter the building without any restrictions, which again raised a question in my mind.

There was no reception on the ground floor and even, no guard. This was a plain looking government office. I took the same lift which Florence or Ganesh, the bulky man, had taken to take me to Prince's office. On reaching the top floor, I found no trace of any office. On the contrary, the rooftop was occupied by discarded furniture, like the other buildings.

I went down using the same lift. Caught hold of the first person whom I saw on ground floor.

"Bhaiya, do you work here"?

"Yes",

"Since how long"?

He was a Haryanvi. As expected, instead of replying straight, came the question "tanne ke karna hai"? (What has it to do with you?)

"Bhai I am looking for the office on the roof top, which was there some four years ago."

"Han', it was a makeshift office of the people who were getting this place renovated."

Again, a shock.

"You mean, it was not a government office"?

"Bawala hai ke? Kaun sa Sarkari office Chhat pe hove se?" (Are you crazy? Which government office works on the rooftop?)

Yes, I was crazy. I had been crazy for the past four years.

I kept thinking that although I had lost my mother and father both, but I was working for my mother land.

But now I was not sure, whom I was working for.

I was working in India House, which was an Indian Government place in London. It cannot be that the entire setup was fake. It cannot be that the entire setup was corrupt.

There had to be an answer to this. And the only person who could provide this answer, was Prince. I was to ask him. Even at the cost of my life.

I left for London, the same night. There was no question of meeting my brother or any family.

In August 2020, Ranjit was visiting London on an official trip. During this trip, he visited India House. He met the Project Brihadratha team. It was just me, Yang and Prince. As I was sure Ranjit was the NSA, this meeting confirmed that I weas working on an Indian Project.

Ranjit gave the details about the developments happening in India on the infrastructure front and how, it was going to help Brihadratha. Brihadratha was not only to secure Indian borders permanently, but it had also to ensure prosperity in India's North-East, North and Tibet.

Kashmir was already undisputed part of India by now. The citizens of Kashmir were happy with the change, as there were economic development and peace in the state, after some three and a half decades.

The work was on for POK. The way Pakistan economy was going, and considering the changes in Kashmir, the day was not far that POK citizens would demand to be merged with India.

The same was the plan for Tibet. But, for that, India had to demonstrate that it will take care of Tibet's economic viability and employment.

Till now, Tibet was considered a burden on Chinese economy. This could have been deliberate, as there was no co-operation intended by the Tibetans.

Tibetans in India were being trained for any types of jobs, for the last four years. The plan was to develop Tibet as a tourist destination. India could help, as numerous Indians queued up to visit Kailash Mansarovar, but were denied Visa by Chinese authorities.

Tibet had a lot to offer to tourists. Under the present circumstances, this aspect was not explored. Visiting Tibet under Chinese rule was a pain. If the things could be made right, with their minimalist lifestyle of Tibetans, Tibet could sustain from Tourism alone.

That is what, the Indian government had in mind. There were large number of Buddhists, who wanted to visit Tibet. There were also large number of Hindus, who wanted to visit Mount Kailash. Presently the Chinese policies and high costs of Visa and other taxes discouraged the tourists. If it were to be controlled by Tibetans, this would be the right revenue for them.

Ranjit also updated about the status of infrastructure progress. The construction of New Road to Kailash had already begun. The aim was to link Dharchula in Uttarakhand district with Lipulekh pass, which was the gateway into China from India. Kailash was just 65 kilometers from this pass.

Once Tibet is independent, it would take just about a month to connect Lipulekh with Kailash, through Mansarovar.

After the meeting with Ranjit, there was a meeting called by Prince, as now was the time to work fast on Brihadratha.

I was still skeptical of what to believe coming from Prince, but as this project would solely be driven by Prince. Hence had to listen.

When Prince started explaining Brihadratha, he made it clear that the project executers would be on their own with no connection with Indian government. The project would be controlled remotely, hence none of the agents connected with it would get exposed. We were expected to ensure financial troubles for China, as well as shifting the business to India.

This was the non-violent way to control China.

Prince also shared about Project Wall. While USA, UK along with Pakistan were ensuring an attack on China, we had to be careful not to get entangled into their trap. We can help Project Wall agents with information, but that is where we had to draw the line.

During the next one hour, Prince also explained that Brihadratha is a project which has buy-in from the governments of the USA, the UK and European Union, but none would want to be seen associated with it. While they all will support and would appreciate the final outcome of the project, in case we fail, it would be termed as a project by a few rogue agents.

I still had a looming disbelief around Prince. Perhaps Prince sensed that and after the meeting, when Yang left, he had a detailed discussion with me.

Prince started; "I am impressed with your work. Quite an exciting, on your own decisions, you have been taking".

I was taken aback. Did he know about the Anita episode? It could not be.

There was no point taking a lead and answering, so I kept quiet. I waited if there was anything else coming my way.

"I can see your attention is divided, it's high time I guess, you should know the truth".

I kept quiet. I wanted to wait, to know where this conversation was going. Let Prince say what he wanted to share before I ask my questions.

Prince continued – "for starters, let me assure you that you are and have been working on a project, which has approval from the Indian Government".

So, he knew about my doubts. There was no point in wondering, how? By now, I was aware that every report reaches the agency. It could be the Haryanvi at Vayu Sena Bhavan or Yang or my mannerism, which would have alerted Prince.

Seeing me confused, Prince continued – "don't worry. We have not installed any bugs or, we do not have any analysers to read your thoughts. It is natural, that I met you last in the makeshift office at Vayu Sena Bhavan, then in India House, my estate and now with today's statements, you would be wondering about the same."

Prince continued – "we never had any meetings at the office of RAW, as told just now, I am leading a separate group, which cannot be linked to RAW".

Prince continued – "Operation Brihadratha along with Project Wall, are operations being contributed to, by many countries. I was with RAW and have been chosen for this operation for my proximity with external intelligence agencies of most countries. It is also true, that I was first chosen by CIA to lead this operation, however later, the Indian Government having not liked the ways of CIA, separated themselves from the project. Ralph

Stevens is the head now for Project Wall and I am managing Brihadratha. We are extending help to each other"

I knew that India and most Asian countries were sick of China's expansionism policy. India was aware that China was growing its influence in Indian Ocean, by funding smaller countries like Sri Lanka, Pakistan, Maldives, Nepal, Bangladesh etc., which in turn was a move to surround India from all directions. Had India refused to participate in this mission, the participating countries would have ignored India's interest.

There was a silence for few minutes, during which I evaluated whatever was said.

Overall, it made sense till now.

Prince continued – "I am also aware that now you know, how your parents died. Believe me, this is not how Indian government functions, and there was no role of any Indian agent in this".

"There was a mistake made by Ramkumar, as your unavailability for this mission was mentioned in front of a CIA agent. They took lead, without the consent of Indian Government. We have already lodged a formal protest for that, and we made the CIA agree to the clause that this type of action should not happen anymore. This was another reason, why India separated from Project Wall, as we know, CIA may do this again. Still, we cannot bring your parents back, which is a shame, and we deeply regret this."

Prince took a moment to speak again, allowing me to digest what has been said just now. He could see that I was still not at peace. So, he continued –

"You know, this is between you and me, I am aware about your action against Anita. However, I assure that there will be no further investigation. She will continue to remain missing, as far as the agency records are concerned. I feel that we have erred, and your revenge is justified. For the person issuing orders to Anita, as said earlier, was not from Indian agencies, so no point in dragging this further. It would only do you harm".

This came as a shock.

Till now, I was thinking that no one knew about my taking care of Anita. There were no witnesses. Perhaps I was wrong.

A quick calculation. If the agency or CIA knew about this, they would have ensured by now, a fitting punishment for me, which would have most likely been in a similar manner like Anita.

The reason, I was still free or alive, was just told to me and I had no doubt, this was true.

Prince continued – "you would remember, me telling you not to make any contact with your immediate family. It was for this reason. We never wanted a similar action against any of them. I am happy for your such restrain, and till now, there has been no communication between you, your brother, and his family. In their own interest, please keep it that way, till Brihadratha is over. For now, they have been told that you are missing in action, later, we can arrange your return."

I wanted to say that I missed my niece, but was not sure, if I should be sharing my emotions any further. So, I kept quiet.

Prince allowed me to finish my tea, then looked at me, if I had any further questions.

One thing was clear, there was nothing hidden from him, and what he was asking me, was to leave this pursuit of revenge, for my own good and that of my remaining family. He was asking me to complete Brihadratha successfully, if I wanted to be free again.

It was not said, but there could be a threat, if I do not go ahead with Brihadratha, I would never find peace.

I kept mulling over the discussion on my way back home and for next two days. There was no further contact from anyone or the agency for these two days. Perhaps, The Prince wanted me to have these two days with myself.

After two days, I got a call from Yang. She came to my home. This is when I had some open discussions with Yang, for the first time in my life.

When she left, it was time to start Brihadratha. It was time that we both started working together. She helped me make up my mind. This was the only way out.

Next six years, we dedicated for the build-up, strategizing, planning, hiring, and placing agents. The work was tough and required systematic planning. By the end of 2026, China had lost substantial business to India. Most of their investments abroad made heavy losses.

Moreover, Wang Li, the Chinese President was voted out of power. His economic, social, foreign and religious policies, which were considered outstanding, backfired. This resulted the end of his political career.

By 2028, Tibet and Mongolia became free. They both joined hands with India, which created further problems for China, as now it was surrounded from two sides, by friends of India.

Even Taiwan and South Korea supported India, entrapping the Chinese from three sides.

CHAPTER 17

The new India

India's road infrastructure underwent a significant transformation during the second decade of the third millennium. This emerged as a critical factor in the country's economic growth and social development. India's road network was largely inadequate to support the country's burgeoning population and economic ambitions.

The pre-independence era saw a limited and poorly maintained road system, primarily focused on connecting major cities and ports for colonial trade purposes. Post-independence, the government recognized the need for a robust road infrastructure to spur economic growth and social mobility. However, as the country was marred with growing corruption, this need remained a need.

The turning point came with the change of government in 2014. The new government promised stability and in turn could generate significant investments and policy reforms aimed at expanding and modernizing the road network. The new road projects, aimed to upgrade, rehabilitate, and expand India's national highways network, which forms the backbone of the country's road transportation.

By 2024, an estimated 85,000 km of new highways were developed, focusing on improving road connectivity in border and rural areas, port connectivity, and economic corridors. through Smart Cities Mission, India developed smart roads with features like intelligent traffic management, integrated multimodal transport systems, and pedestrian-friendly pathways.

There was a need to secure India's Borders, and it was found that even after 70 years of independence, the Indian borders lacked proper roads.

India, with its diverse topography and geopolitical landscape, faced unique challenges in securing its borders. The rugged terrains of the Himalayas in the north, the vast deserts of Rajasthan in the west, the dense forests in the northeast, and the expansive coastline required a robust and strategic approach to border management. The lack of roads caused delays during many conflicts with its neighbors. These delays caused fatal for Indian soldiers.

The borders with China and Pakistan have always seen periodic escalations, necessitating rapid military mobilization and logistics support. Improved road infrastructure enabled faster deployment of troops, equipment, and supplies. This could enhance India's defensive and offensive capabilities.

By 2025, India had completed numerous strategic roads, bridges, and tunnels, often under challenging conditions. Atal Tunnel at Rohtang Pass in Himachal Pradesh was built as the world's longest highway tunnel above 10,000 feet. The tunnel provided all-weather connectivity between Manali and the Lahaul-Spiti valley, significantly reducing travel time for military and civilian purposes.

Zojila Tunnel was constructed to provide year-round connectivity between Srinagar and Leh, crucial for the strategic Ladakh region. This tunnel ensured uninterrupted supply chains and military readiness, even during harsh winter months.

The north-eastern region, shares borders with China, Myanmar, Bhutan, and Bangladesh. North-East Road Network was a significant infrastructure development move. This move was aimed to improve connectivity and enhance regional security and economic integration in this region. The most important was the New Road to Kailash.

This was the most strategic move, which was aimed, at one side to secure Indian Borders and on the other, economic independence for Tibet.

Mount Kailash and Mansarovar Lake are revered by Hindus, Buddhists, and Jains. Pilgrims have embarked on challenging journeys to these sacred sites for centuries, braving difficult terrains and harsh weather conditions.

Mount Kailash is considered the dwelling place of Lord Shiva in Hinduism, the meditation site of Buddhist saint Milarepa, and a source of cosmic energy for Jains. Lake Mansarovar, located close to the mountain, is believed to be one of the highest freshwater lakes globally and is thought to purify the sins of those who bathe in its waters.

The idea of constructing a new road to Kailash Mansarovar was born out of the need to offer a safer, faster, cheaper, and more convenient route for pilgrims and travelers, while also improving connectivity in the region. However, as it complemented Project Brihadratha, the importance of the road increased.

The new road was inaugurated in June 2026 and linked Dharchula in Uttarakhand to Lipulekh Pass on the India-China border. From Lipulekh, pilgrims could now continue their journey to Kailash Mansarovar through Tibet. The path covers around 80 kilometers, passing through the Pithoragarh district and ascending to the high-altitude Lipulekh Pass.

The construction process involved overcoming numerous challenges, the major one, when Nepal under the influence of China, started claiming encroachment to their land. Nepal had a concern of their own. Till now, the Kailash Mansarovar Yatra happened through Nepal, which was a revenue generator for them. Now, with this alternate route, Indian could go directly to Mount Kailash.

It took two years for Indian government, to convince Nepal that there was no encroachment. And when the new route began, more Indian and foreign tourists started using the route, generating innumerable revenue generation opportunities for Indians and Tibetans. Similarly, for Nepal as well, now their scenic towns of Limi, Bhimdutta and Hilsa could be accessed by this road, which helped generate more revenue through tourism.

The next challenge was with China, which did not allow entry to Indian public through Lipulekh initially. But when the Indian government restricted travel to Kailash for two full years, China had to bend. Their business and economy were going south anyway.

The new road had made the pilgrimage more accessible to a larger number of people, including elderly and physically challenged individuals, who were previously unable to undertake the arduous journey. This allowed more devotees to fulfill their spiritual aspirations and deepen their connection with the sacred sites.

Additionally, the improved connectivity boosted tourism in the region, leading to economic growth and development. Local communities witnessed an increase in income and employment opportunities, as the influx of pilgrims and tourists created a demand for accommodation, transportation, and other services.

Almost 70% of the new road was an all-weather road. This concept, India experimented for all border roads.

An all-weather road was a road, which was first made and then covered by a concrete roof, like the shape of a tunnel. The given idea was that all weather roads can allow travel without the worry of snow, rain, land slide or any other calamity. The main reason behind this type of construction was that the traffic movement or movement of troops could not be detected, even by high resolution satellite cameras.

Earlier, the pilgrims had to travel more than 1500 KM through China controlled Tibet. With this new road, Lipulekh pass was just over 550 KMs from Delhi, which could be travelled in 10 hours. From Lipulekh, Mount Kailash was another 65 KMs.

This opened door of economy, for Tibet, which the Tibetan spiritual leader was worried about.

The all-weather road also proved beneficial towards liberation of Tibet.

CHAPTER

Wang

In 2015, Wang rose to the position of President of China after serving as the vice president for ten years. During his time as vice president, he successfully propelled China's economy to unprecedented heights.

Having been elected as the General Secretary of the Chinese Communist Party by a narrow margin, many criticized Wang's policies as draconian, inhumane, and anti-establishment. However, majority of Communist Party members had to acknowledge his outstanding work during his tenure as vice president, which led to significant economic growth in China.

The situation was critical as India, China's neighboring country, had a new Prime Minister who was gaining popularity worldwide. This posed a potential threat to China's economic dominance. If India's power continued to grow, China would have to reconsider its expansion policies.

China's economic expansionism was accompanied by a controversial strategy to extend its influence across Asia, the Middle East, Europe, and Africa. China aimed to deepen economic ties with partner countries and strategically advance its geopolitical interests through massive infrastructure projects and generous loans.

China's Belt and Road Initiative was a vast infrastructure development project that spanned multiple continents, including Asia, Africa, and Europe. China promoted this initiative as a means to enhance connectivity, promote trade, and foster economic development. However, what China did not disclose was that this initiative was also aimed at expanding its global influence and soft power.

While Belt and Road projects provided much-needed infrastructure development, the countries agreeing to these projects miscalculated high interest rates and stringent repayment conditions attached to Chinese loans. As a result, partner countries became heavily indebted to China and faced the risk of losing strategic assets if they failed to repay their loans.

In the Middle East, China heavily invested in infrastructure projects such as ports, railways, and energy facilities. However, China's economic engagement in the region had geopolitical implications as it sought to secure access to energy resources, expand its market presence, and counterbalance Western influence. Moreover, the Middle East took note about a new law introduced by Wang in China. In China, Muslims were a minority. The new law barred any Chinese to practice any religion apart from communism. This was again a mistake made by Wang. No government should ever suppress the practice of any religion. The

Muslim countries saw this as a direct attack on their religion. Even the fundamentalists in the trusted ally Pakistan, pledged to take revenge.

China's presence in Europe had grown significantly, with investments in infrastructure, technology, and manufacturing sectors. Eastern and Southern European countries embraced Chinese investment as a means to stimulate economic growth and modernize their infrastructure. However, Western European countries and the European Union expressed concerns about certain clauses in the agreements that could potentially allow China to take over.

Overall, China's economic expansionism and Belt and Road Initiative had both positive and negative consequences for partner countries, with some benefitting from infrastructure development while others facing the risk of heavy debt and loss of strategic assets. However, the challenges for Wang increased every day, as now, with India emerging as a leader, the partner countries had an option, which was not to the benefit of China.

By 2020, Wang and the entire Chinese National People's Congress realized the speed of economic growth in India. China had taken advantage of India's weak road infrastructure, which helped them with an advantage during conflicts. China was well aware that India's ongoing improvement of road infrastructure would not only enhance border management but also pose a constant threat to China's economy. Better road infrastructure meant better business and a stronger economy for any country.

Now with Kashmir issue resolved, Kashmiris started exporting tons of fresh fruits, vegetables, dry fruits, and herbs. This benefitted them, as well as the Indian economy. With the new road, rail and air infrastructure, the transportation of these perishable goods was much easier.

Additionally, Wang received information from the Chinese secret service, MSS, about growing unrest in Tibet. The sentiments of freedom were being fueled by a few mercenaries, causing restlessness in the region. Furthermore, there was discontent within the People's Congress regarding the excessive spending to maintain control over Tibet. Wang knew that he couldn't suppress this restlessness for much longer.

That's when they began putting their questionable policies into action. Numerous countries found themselves trapped in China's debt. It was now the perfect opportunity to seize control of their assets. Wang gradually deployed the Chinese Army in these countries. This increased the Chinese sentiments in his favor, but it also added to the expenses.

Chinese investments were already under significant impact in Europe, America, and Africa, but due to COVID, the economies of these nations were in shambles. Furthermore, these countries had suspicions that China was behind the creation of COVID and the suffering of people worldwide. With all this in mind, withdrawing investments from these countries would have had dire consequences.

The only alternative left was to negate the popularity of India, which would buy some time for Wang, till China makes it next move.

So, first, it was a direct media attack on Purshottam group of companies. When it failed, Wang thought of reviving operation Shoelace, which failed last time. This time, it should not be targeted towards Banks. It should be targeted towards the public.

India had introduced digital payment methods. Their UPI was a success and one of its kind in the world. How about exploiting this?

Shoelace was a success this time. During the next three years, Indian public lost billions of dollars. This was a straight gain to China. But again, Indians are the best brains in the world, as far as the technology is concerned. The actions taken by the Indians contributed towards the negative impact and downfall of Wang

Towards the end of 2025, MSS informed Wang about a probable terrorism attack on Beijing. It was suspected that the attack was being planned by Pakistan along with some Islamic countries, as China had banned Islam.

CHAPTER 19

The Conflict

The third decade of the third millennium started on a negative foot. It started with COVID Pandemic, which lasted for two full years. The next two years saw various conflicts and wars between nations.

War takes on many forms, extending far beyond the traditional battlefields. It encompasses conflicts of various types, each with its own origins and objectives.

The third millennium warfare saw, physical warfare between nations like Russia and Ukraine, as well as Israel and Palestine. War within Syria as well as, American forces exiting Afghanistan which escalated Muslim population exodus from these Muslim-dominated countries. The citizens of these countries took refuge in peaceful and developed European countries. Soon started striving for equal rights, which gave one a reason to believe, this is a well-orchestrated move. The refugees soon started their attempts to convert residents through means, such as rape or marriages, which looked like an attempt of the ultimate goal of establishing a global Muslim rule.

This decade saw a unique kind of war, which was a war to establish economic supremacy. This war commenced with COVID19. Unlike the other wars, this war was behind the scenes, away from the traditional battlegrounds. The ultimate objective remained the same as the previous wars: world domination.

Away from all this, India under the new leadership started emerging as a trusted ally.

While China was blamed as the creator of COVID19, India stood out by developing three vaccines to combat it. Not only did India successfully control the spread of the virus domestically, but it also provided vaccines to countries in need, free of charge. This shift in dynamics led to countries favoring direct investments in India over China.

Consequently, countries refrained from further investments in China, leading to a significant economic downturn for the latter. This decline in China's economy worked in India's favor, as the world began to view India as a reliable friend compared to China, which was perceived as exploitative and aggressive.

Gradually, countries like the United States, Russia, and others started looking towards India as a potential ally to counter China's unchecked expansion.

By now, Indians were at the helm of major multinational corporations worldwide. The United Kingdom, once a global superpower and former colonizer of India, now had an Indian Prime Minister. The United States had an

Indian Vice President, with strong indications that the next President would also be Indian. Even if that didn't come to pass, it was certain that the new American President would be heavily influenced by Indian leadership.

Additionally, India had forged strong friendships with powerful nations, some of which were bitter enemies with each other, but all considered India a friend. India maintained positive relationships with Iran and Iraq, as well as Saudi Arabia and the entire Middle East, including Israel.

Despite China's heavy debt hold on the African continent, India helped African countries in their development initiatives, particularly in agriculture and water resources. India's agreements with Africa, providing billions in concessional credit for agriculture and water projects, helped the continent regain its self-sufficiency and transition from *aid recipients to trading partners.*

As India was becoming a clear threat to China, it was natural for China to find ways to retaliate. Now, the war between India and China was physical, as well as on economic front.

On the physical front, there were skirmishes on the Sino Indian borders in the Northeast and North. Earlier, the skirmishes were not retaliated and excursions by China were not challenged, as India lacked proper infrastructure. Now in the present regime, the new government created an outstanding infrastructure for the Army.

Since 2015, a proper demarcation of borders highlighting the areas encroached by China and Pakistan, helped the Indian Army consolidate its positions. Proper and smooth road network on the borders, ensured swift movement of vehicles, also ensured the army the adequate help, in the hour of need.

India also constructed aircraft landing fields, which further ensured timely help. The aircraft fields enabled supply of fresh groceries to the men on the front, too. Earlier, they had to live on canned foods, which often crossed their expiry even at the time of supply. This further boosted the morale of the Indian Army.

Next, the Indian Prime Minister made it a point, not only to visit the borders regularly to motivate the soldiers, but also to spend quality time with them in their bunkers.

This was a first for any top leader of the country. During his visits, the Prime Minister reiterated the support for the soldiers. No matter what, they, or in their absence, their families will be looked after well.

The defense ministry was also instructed to allow the men on ground to take their decisions and not impose their own decisions, which they took sitting in the comfort of their offices.

This was new for China as well, as since the year 1963, they kept treating this area as their own.

There was a different India as well, as far as the border with Pakistan was concerned.

In the year 1948, while the Indian government was still consolidating its states post partition with Pakistan, Pakistan forces entered in Kashmir and illegally occupied a large portion of land, which they started claiming their own. For India, it remained as Pakistan Occupied Kashmir or POK for short.

Similarly in the year 1962, Chinese forces started encroaching the north Indian border, establishing their hold on Aksai Chin and started claiming the Northeastern state of Arunachal Pradesh, as part of Tibet, which was already encroached by them. These northeastern and northern territories became disputed since those days.

In the year 2015, the Indian government, while finalizing the Indian map, brought POK and Aksai Chin and as integral part of India and declared it criminal, should anyone display the Indian map minus these areas.

In the year 2019, Indian government took a step further by eradicating Article 370 from Indian Constitution, which earlier provided special status to Kashmir being a disputed territory. By removing this article, India made a statement and a clear claim to the entire Kashmir, including POK.

While Pakistan was under the impression that the Muslim countries would support them on this Indian move, United Arab Emirates UAE, became the first country to support this Indian move. Later, Saudi Arabia, Kuwait, Qatar, Bahrain, Turkey, Oman, Riyad, all pitched in their support for this Indian move.

Next move was, now if the BBC or any such channels talked about POK, India retaliated by using the phrases like Pakistan occupied Baluchistan, Pakistan occupied Sindh, China occupied Tibet or China occupied Mongolia. Some Indian media also started using the phrases like British occupied Ireland, Scotland, Whales etc., which was a fact on the same grounds.

The strong government in India continued growing its influence economically and politically. It affected China adversely, with the same proportion. The investments, which were attracted by China earlier, were now going the Indian way. Even the developed countries like United States, United Kingdom, Russia, France, Israel, Saudi Arabia etc. started favoring India over China.

This was when the first covert economic attack came towards India, in the form of Kindle Guard report.

In the year 2022, Kindle Guard Corporation, which was an investment research firm and had substantial investments from China, claimed that they had short positions in India's Purshottam group of companies, which has been allowed by the Indian regulators.

Purshottam group companies had grown to become the largest conglomerate in India over the last 20 years and had been attracting major foreign direct investments over the last decade.

Due to these investments and growth in the companies associated with the group, stock prices skyrocketed, and the stocks were traded at all international exchanges at unbelievable volumes and rates.

Soon after the report was released, the Group companies experienced an acute decline in their share prices. By the end of June 2022, the group lost over $100 billion in value.

The attack was not only limited to the group, but it also raised serious concerns on the accounting and regulatory aspects of Indian companies. This was bad news, as the markets ran on sentiments. While there were clear indications that the report was motivated on the behest of a stock manipulator, further investments in Purshottam group reached rock bottom.

By the end of September quarter, India saw an overall decline in foreign investment by almost 16%.

The regulatory authorities in India, United States, United Kingdom etc. issued statements, not to believe the report, as it was prepared by a short seller, who himself had claimed to be on the wrong side of law. But the support to the report by Hong Kong, China etc., clearly indicated, on whose behest, the misleading report was published.

Due to the allegations, American, Swiss, and Chinese finance companies and banks stopped accepting bonds and Bank Guarantees of Purshottam group companies as collateral for margin loans to its private banking clients.

They also reduced their exposure in other Indian companies, for almost a year.

The allegations of Kindle Guard were proved to be baseless during independent investigations. Still, it took almost a year for Indian companies to regain the trust of the investors.

By mid-May of 2023, the investments started afresh in Indian companies, indicating a renewed faith.

Next came the sponsoring of the Digital Payment Frauds. In 2016, India changed its physical currency to control black money and Pakistan sponsored terrorism through Indian forged currency. This was the time when the government encouraged digital money and transactions through digital means.

The global economists made fun of India on this move. They felt that India having 70% of its population in the rural areas with minimal internet connectivity, how would digital transactions be able to benefit Rural consumers.

By 2020, when the COVID pandemic enforced lockdowns with no access to banks, the government supported digital transactions in a big way. By 2021, the digital payment transactions reached the remotest area in India. Various digital payment aggregators started operating in India and an estimated 27% business shifted online. There were online stores for clothes, food, equipment, shoes, electronics, which delivered straight to home of the consumer. The payment for the products delivered was received online. Now, Indians could get items of their choice including food, 24/7. This was a big leap for the Indian business. Not only this, platforms like Unified Payments Interface (UPI), mobile wallets, and internet banking became ubiquitous, making transactions faster and more convenient.

With the growth of opportunity came the opportunity of fraud as well. Cybercriminals leveraged from sophisticated techniques to exploit vulnerabilities in digital payment systems, leading to significant financial losses for individuals and businesses. Soon, it was evident that digital payment frauds were originating from bordering countries.

There was a surge of Digital Payment Frauds like sending fraudulent messages and calls impersonating legitimate financial institutions or payment platforms, to steal sensitive information or just sending a fraudulent payment link to receive payment and then defrauding the public. There were Malware Attacks, deployment of malicious software to capture personal and financial data from users' devices. Fake Apps and Websites were created to deceive users into divulging their credentials or making payments. This all was a part of cross border terrorism, aimed towards psychological impact and erosion of trust in digital payment systems, which was successfully launched by Indian government.

Soon, the loss through digital payment frauds accounted for losses exceeding billions of dollars. Small businesses and individual users reported losing significant sums to these sophisticated fraud schemes. The prevalence of fraud made many users skeptical of digital payment platforms, hindering the adoption of cashless transactions. Businesses relying on digital payments faced disruptions due to decreased consumer confidence and heightened security concerns.

India's Strategic Response team recognized the threat posed by these frauds, particularly those linked to state-sponsored actors. The Indian government, in collaboration with financial institutions and technology companies, initiated a multi-pronged strategy to safeguard its digital economy.

It is said that people who live in glass houses should not throw stones on others. How true it was in this case. It was time for India to give a befitting response to its neighbors. While Pakistan was already down on economy. China should also feel the pinch.

China's entire trade surplus was parked abroad unlike India. It was time for India to retaliate, but not openly, in the same covert way.

CHAPTER 20

Ismail and Faridah

They both were first cousins, who were engaged to be married, when Yang met them in the MI8 academy in 2017. While Faridah was a UK citizen by birth, Ismail's idea of marrying her was more towards getting a UK citizenship. They both had their own reasons for joining Project Wall. Not everything they told each other or to others was true.

It was true that Ali, Faridah's father ran a video cassette library in South Hall. It was true that Faridah had four sisters and two brothers, and her mother was a UK citizen by birth. The point which Faridah did not share with anyone was that when her father Ali was deported the fourth time, he was only taken back by the UK government to help them solve the London bombing case of 2011.

All these four times when Faridah's father was deported, he helped the UK government some way or the other to get an extended stay in the UK. This fourth time, when he returned, the task was much more difficult and unethical. It was to give evidence against three innocent Pakistanis, his own countrymen.

By now, Ali was wiser and in exchange for becoming a key witness in the London Bombing case, he asked for permanent citizenship and a government job. As per the immigration law, he could have got the citizenship long ago due to his marriage with Faridah's mom, but every time he was completing the mandatory period of stay, he got involved in some violation or the other, to miss the citizenship and inviting deportation.

The evidence provided by Ali, resulted in electric chair for his three countrymen, but that was fine by him, as now no one could send him back to Pakistan. Moreover, he could also get his brother's son to London basis official documents cleared by the UK government.

He had already passed the official age for a government job, so the UK government promised a job for one of his daughters, and his brother's son.

This is how Faridah and Ismail were selected, first for sponsored education, and later for a job with the government. The story given to Ali and his wife was that they worked different government jobs, while the truth was, they were recruited by MI8.

Ismail had a fundamental upbringing in Pakistan. While Faridah was more tolerant. Being with Ismail for over a year, fundamentalism rubbed off good on Faridah as well. Faridah was also ashamed of her father's actions due to which three Muslims lost their life. Hence, was determined to do something good, for the Muslim community.

Ismail often used to discuss about the miseries the Muslims undergo in China, and something should be done for that. By then China had already started sending the practicing Muslims to labor camps. The government had already started converting the mosques to shopping malls or educational institutions. They had already started banning the practice of any religion, mandating communism the only religion to be followed in China. Faridah, now a devout Muslim, agreed with Ismail.

These feelings and beliefs were to be used by the CIA, when the time came. But as they had to stay together, they had to convince their parents by getting married.

The marriage was just to put their parents at ease. For their parents, they both had steady government jobs. The parents didn't care much about what the children did, as far as they were on their own.

During 2016-2018, Prince was managing a larger plan, which included CIA, MI8 and other agencies. Soon, Ismail and Faridah were MI8 counterparts managed by Ralph. They chose their own way to teach China a lesson, which was based on their religious belief.

For Ismail and Faridah, visiting Pakistan was easy, as they had their roots there. Ismail's father was in Peshawar owning a wholesale business of flowers. He was rich and connected but was often troubled by the ISI.

Ismail was concerned with this and hence discussed it with Ralph. Ralph not only discussed Ismail's cause with his ISI counterpart, but also got Ismail in touch with an ISI agent.

When Ismail and Faridah were assigned to Project Wall, their task was already decided. They were hard liner agents, unlike what Yang and Adwait were to do. Their handlers in MI8 had devised a plan for them. As far as Prince was concerned, his task with them was only coordination. Prince had to provide support in case Faridah and Ismail needed.

Yang had worked in Beijing for many years. She knew Beijing as back of her hand, especially the important buildings including the National Peoples' Congress building. She knew each nook and corner. She knew which part of the building was vulnerable and accessible to which type of people. This entire knowledge was shared by Yang with Faridah and Ismail.

Although, it was already over ten years now, but Yang still had kept many contacts in Beijing. The one difficulty they had in hand was that Faridah and Ismail were not having Mongolian features. So, although they could travel to China as tourists, they could never stay there for long, and they could also not visit the country frequently, as it would raise alerts with security agencies.

By now, Pakistan had already realized that the Belt and Road project touted by China as for Pakistan's growth, was nothing but a debt trap. While China was getting access through the entire Pakistan by way of China – Pakistan Economic Corridor, the meager $1.5 billion investment in Pakistan's infra projects by China was a sham. China was investing in building Railways, Roadways, Electric power generation plants and other infra projects in Pakistan, but this all came with a clause of takeover, in an event of default. This sounded big trouble, as this meant handing over the control of Pakistan, to China, should Pakistan default in repayments.

On the other hand, Pakistan government knew that their internal policies and corrupt government officials will never allow repayment to happen. Their economic condition, however, did not allow them to reject these clauses in the investment agreements. Hence, Pakistan signed those agreements, but also joined hands with the MI8 to help in Project Wall.

When the project started, ISI being extremely qualified for planting explosives in public places, this was the task assigned to them. The ISI was tasked to first smuggle the RDX, detonators and other raw material to a remote location in China, from where specially trained men and women will assemble the explosives and plant at various locations.

The remote location was chosen as Kashgar, which was a Muslim dominated area in China on Karakorum Highway, the highway which linked Pakistan with

China. The Muslims in Kashgar were suppressed, so they agreed to help fellow Muslims of Pakistan.

Ismail's father owned wholesale flowers business in Peshawar. For this, he used to procure some 80 varieties of flowers locally from Peshawar and from Gilgit, Baltistan.

Till recently, the locally grown flowers were used for local ceremonies like weddings, funerals, and other functions. With the China's Belt and Road initiative, Pakistan saw an opportunity and their counsellor in China, persuaded a deal called, Pakistan – China Floriculture Cooperation.

China aimed to grow its exports of flowers products like, essential oil, flower jam and cosmetics. Under this cooperation, it agreed to share the expertise with Pakistan. In return, Pakistan would export their home grown such products, which will help China enhance their exports. This was touted as an international business opportunity by Pakistan, which benefitted both the countries.

Ismail's father joined the wagon.

Ralph had introduced Ismail to an ISI agent. Now, that agent and Ismail aimed to utilize this opportunity, to smuggle RDX along with flowers. This meant Ismail's shifting base to Peshawar along with his wife, as the business was slated to grow. This was not liked by Faridah's father, but he had to bend.

It started slow, but within a year, the business started blooming, just like the flowers. Flowers being perishable, the export was usually by air, which was costly. A solution for this arrived at by the two governments. On Pakistan's proposal, China allowed opening of various process centers in Kashgar, Xinjiang District of China.

Through Karakorum highway, the distance between Gilgit and Kashgar was reduced to some 700 odd kilometers, which could be covered by trucks in less than 12 hours. Opening of these process centers, was hence an important step, towards this cooperation.

This was also an important step, as far as Ismail's mission was concerned in project Wall. While Faridah joined the business, they both ensured that in the entire truckloads of flowers, a few boxes of RDX were kept.

These boxes were handed over separately by the truck drivers at a remote house before entering Kashgar. The recipients were specially trained operatives, trained by Jon Russel.

Slowly the stock of explosives started building up. The Gilgit – Kashgar highway was operational only between May and October and during the first year, there were already a few tons of RDX stored in a cave close to Kashgar.

CHAPTER 21

Kashgar

March 20, 2022. There was a message received by Ismail on his phone, which stated "this is a message from Ismail Yusuf Bank, Karachi. Your account is going to be deactivated, as there is an outstanding amount of Rupees 5000 to be paid. To avoid deactivation of account, may click on following link" https://NPh1RokhN6JS.PK=1.

There had been many digital payments frauds prevalent during those days, wherein the gullible people were taken to unsolicited sites, which lead them to sharing of their confidential bank details and then their accounts were cleaned by fraudsters. At first glance this message appeared to be a similar con message to Ismail. However, he knew that the suffix, 'PK=1' was not so unsolicited. This message was from his friends in ISI.

He went to a secure computer to click on the link. The link took him to a video conferencing call. Shahbaz, from ISI was on the other side.

Shahbaz was from the technological surveillance team. His team's job was to monitor communications over the internet. The team had developed specialized tools to decipher the strongest encrypted communications, even up to 256 bits, which is the military grade encryption.

Shahbaz did not waste any time and shared with Ismail to be cautious. He had come across some communications, which were apparently between two Chinese MSS agents. The agents apparently were discussing the emergence of some security threats in Kashgar.

This was sufficient for Ismail to be extra cautious. Kashgar was a sleepy town. There were no reasons for any alert being generated, if not for the actions supervised by Ismail. It was time for counter action.

Kashgar had been of historical importance, as the province has been a trading centre since ages. Situated at the foot of the Pamirs mountains, Kashgar was an important point of the famed Silk Route, connecting Europe via Uzbekistan, as well as with Kashmir valley.

Kashgar was occupied by Chinese at the end of the 2nd century BCE, taking it from the Yuezhi people. In 752 Kashgar was taken over by the Turks, thereafter by Uighurs and then the Mongols. Between 1862 to 1875, Kashgar was a centre of the Muslim Rebellion and became the capital of the Muslim general Yakub Beg. Another Muslim rebellion, led by Ma Zhongyang, took place in the area from 1928 to 1943 but was finally suppressed by China with Soviet aid. Since 1943, the land is under Chinese control, under the Chinese central government.

Being a Muslim dominated area, there was a commonality on religious beliefs between the citizens of Kashgar and Pakistan, hence Ismail could get many volunteers here, to help in his cause. Slowly, when the RDX stocks started to increase, more people were sent from Gilgit, by Gilgit – Kashgar bus service. The raw RDX was to be converted into remote control devises.

The majority of population in Kashgar practiced Islam till as late as 2017, when the Chinese government banned practice of religion. The ban was a result of an official report, stating that there are some 3000 ISIS terrorists active in China, working to establish Sharia.

The Chinese government issued an official notification banning practice of any sort of religion. For Chinese, the official religion was declared as Communism. As a result of this notification, the government started shutting down mosques, and shifting the practicing Muslims to correctional camps.

There were many Kashgar residents, who felt suppressed for not being able to practice their religion. They all happily became associates of Ismail led group and provided space to fellow Muslims, who set up laboratories for "extracting oils from flowers". Side by side the group started creating explosive devices, to be used later.

Mohammad Xuing Hua was a Kashgar Muslim, who was the contact point of Ismail. He was overlooking the shifting and storage of explosives, in a secluded cave on the Karakoram highway, on the outskirts of Kashgar town. Hua was earlier an active ISIS agent and when the crackdown on Mosques started in 2017, he shifted base to Kashgar and started working as a transport operator. He changed his name to Hua Xuing, abandoning Mohammad from his name.

It was apparent to Ismail, that either Hua or one of his men went soft on caution, resulting in this alert.

Ismail had to act fast. Staying in Peshawar, he estimated that the Kashgar cave would have some eleven tons of explosives. It had taken them five years to transport that stuff under disguise. There was no way it could go wasted. It was not clear if MSS was aware about the storage place. And there was no time to waste to gain this knowledge.

The cave where the explosives were stored was just before entering Kashgar. Even though the storage was accessible by transport, still, shifting that entire load could raise another alert.

Ismail had a plan ready. He knew Yang had good connections in MSS. He had to seek a favor from Yang.

Ismail sent an encrypted message to Hua, to shift about half a ton of explosive to Id Kah Mosque, that same night. The Id Kah Mosque was now a tourist place after 2017, as no form of worship was allowed.

The job was tough. It was already late evening in Kashgar. As Hua could not depend on anyone, he took out a small truck by himself, to shift the stuff. Shifting of half a ton of explosives meant shifting of 25 boxes, each weighing 20 Kgs.

Hua had been an active ISIS operative, but the last five years of idleness had made him futile. It was only by the early next morning, he could reach Id Kah, along with his truck.

Now, he had to park that truck and wait. It was time for Fajr, the first prayer of the day. It pained him to see no activity at the mosque. Still, he sensed some unnatural movement within the mosque.

He opened the truck door, and stepped out, closing the door behind. Being a trained operative, he was alert. Still pretending having a casual walk, he went towards the tea shop near the mosque and ordered a tea. His trained eyes were everywhere, noticing each movement. There definitely was something abnormal around the mosque.

A girl was approaching his truck. She was carrying something in her hand. What? he could not see.

She passed his truck from behind, but his alert gaze could see that whatever she was carrying, was not there when she emerged from behind.

Suddenly, there were two men approaching the tea shop. He started to get up, but the man on the next seat, told him not to. He felt something sharp, pricking his thigh. Then, everything started moving in slow motion.

He could see the man on the next seat getting up, paying his bill and then leaving. The men approaching the tea shop coming nearer. One of the two men searched his pockets, found the truck keys. Took them, then asked him to come with them. Seeing him dazed, left him and started towards the truck on their own.

There was a deafening blast and he noticed pieces of the two men flying. This was the last he saw, before his eyes closed with the final breath.

By afternoon that day, Ismail sent an encrypted thanks to Yang.

Next six months, there were active searches in Kashgar. This meant no risky transportation. The MSS searched every house and commercial premises but found no more explosives. In the search, they found some 100+ sympathizers, who were sent to correctional camps. This was quite a setback to Ismail's operations. But the induced blast helped him as a cover, and when Shahbaz did not find any other activity over the secured communication, they knew it was time to start again.

Transportation of flowers continued. Apart from Hua and Ismail, no one knew about the secret cave storing the explosives. Ismail made it a point not to visit Kashgar during this time.

With Hua gone, he had to find someone to lead the operations.

Raihan Yusra, the girl who had planted a detonator to the explosives laden truck of Hua was the ideal choice. But since she was very young, Ismail started searching for someone experienced. He made his first visit after the Kashgar blasts in October 2026.

He visited the perfumery labs to have business discussions. The lab owners complained about the quality of flowers, and that they could not extract much oil from this quality. Ismail promised to look into this personally and then reduced the rates a notch, to please the buyers.

Ismail could find a few of the people speaking Urdu, along with the Kashgar language Uyghur, which is similar to Persian or Turkish, mixed with Russian. This is the set of people Ismail was looking for.

Ismail started adding these Urdu speaking people to his list of associates. While the local Kashgar Muslims were now trained to create explosive devises, Ismail identified Xian Hazara, a distant cousin of Hua who inherited the transport business, as the one to lead the operation. Hazara's job was to transport the finished devises to Beijing and other important cities of China.

By March 2027, the finished devices were shifted to Beijing and other cities. It was time to start the action.

Beijing, Monday April 07, 2027

It was at 06.50 AM, seven powerful explosions, one after the other, destroyed major portion of Central Business District of Beijing, China. Beijing CBD, as it is called, occupies four square KM of the Chaoyang District, on the east side of Beijing city. And within minutes, it was only dust, smoke and vacuum, due to the massive explosions.

At 07:30 AM, there was another, equally deadly explosion near the Great Hall of the People, some eight KMs from CBD. Although the entire hall was destroyed, there were no casualties, primarily due to the early morning hours on a Sunday. Thankfully, the annual session of the National People's Congress had just concluded last week, else, by this time the staff of legislatures would have started coming in and the casualties would have been massive.

By the day end, there were 27 other massive explosions in various districts and cities of China, including Wuhan, Shanghai, Chongqing and Tianjin.

Beijing had been warned repeatedly by various internal security agencies, that an attack was inevitable. There were many countries, which had a grudge against China. This grudge grew over the last couple of years, culminating to this attack.

Beijing had planned, prepared and practiced its emergency response, but no one was ready for such a mass destruction. Emergency planners within China had prepared themselves for the past couple of months to put in place effective plans to respond to a terrorist attack or other major or catastrophic incident. On April 07, 2027, these plans were put to the test comprehensively for the first time. Hundreds of people from the department of emergency, transport, health and other services worked to rescue the injured and also to see if there were any further casualties, while looking through the rubble of the destroyed properties.

The bombers were later confirmed to be Muslim extremists. 30-year-old Mohammad Suhail Khan, 24-year-old Tanweer Hasib, 19 year old Shahbaz Husain and Hussain Ali was only 18 years old. All four bombers were found to be residents of Kashgar and said to be leading normal everyday lives, including Khan who was a respected teaching assistant.

CHAPTER 22

The Independence

By 2027, China's global business had plummeted by over 55%, while India experienced a significant boost. More than 40 Chinese Banks had to be closed due to defaults by borrowers. On the other hand, the Indian Prime Minister, who was elected in 2014, had successfully secured a consecutive third term in office. However, things were not that rosy for Wang, the President of China.

In June 2027, Wang lost the trust of the Chinese People's Congress following multiple bomb blasts that caused extensive damage across various districts and cities, including Wuhan, Shanghai, Chongqing, and Tianjin. It became evident that Wang was gradually losing control over national security.

The act of terrorism was a direct consequence of Wang's ill-advised policy of declaring communism as the national religion, which greatly offended the Muslim population. Wang's decision to ban Islam, destroy mosques, and send Muslims to correctional camps proved to be a costly mistake.

It was a fact that the world was grappling with Muslim fundamentalism. Almost the entire Europe, Africa, Russia, America and Asia was occupied by fundamentalists. But these continents had surrendered themselves.

Both India and China had posed resistance against the Muslims.

The resistance by India was moderate, but still it reflected in the year 2024 elections. The Muslims rejected the progressive mindset and development, solely on fundamentalism. The popular government somehow was able to secure a majority, but the decision was for everyone to see.

China being a communist country could suppress fundamentalism by force. However, the statement made through multiple blasts was clear evidence, that the Muslims unite, if you challenge their religion.

Wang's policies also invited a global backlash, as India was able to show the world, how the COVID virus was developed in Wuhan labs and how it was exported abroad. Similarly, the evidence placed for the world was clear, that how China had exploited businesses across the globe, with the sole purpose of hostile takeover and expansion.

The Belt and Road projects had failed when the countries realized the ulterior motive behind the same. When the investment policies were compared with India, Indian policies appeared more progressive and inclusive. Against them, the Chinese policies were proven hostile.

This, in entirety, caused the heavy business loss to China and ultimately resulted in deciding fate of Wang.

In 2023, when Wang named himself the General Secretary for a third term, this had irked many within the Communist Party, as this was against the tradition. The tradition mandated the General secretary to hand over power within a decade.

So, Wang was voted out 2926 to 26, in December 2027.

As soon as he was removed from office, armed guards were stationed at Wang's official residence, and since then, he was never seen in public.

The aftermath of Wang's removal from office was a period of uncertainty and instability for China. The damage was too big to repair. The country's economy suffered greatly as global investors lost confidence in its leadership and business relations with other nations deteriorated. The plummeting global business was a direct result of the lack of trust in China's ability to maintain stability and security.

By now, the infrastructure projects, which Indian Prime Minister had started in 2014, were all complete. Although there was resistance from the Muslims, still the educated ones favored him as a leader. His charisma in the global leadership had been proven time and again, which helped him gain the trust of the world leaders. This all played a crucial role in the country's significant boost.

The Prime Minister's policies focused on economic growth, attracting foreign investments, and strengthening diplomatic ties with other nations. India became a preferred destination for businesses looking to expand their operations, leading to a surge in economic activity and job creation.

With China's decline and India's rise, the global power dynamics began to shift. India emerged as a key player in international affairs, gaining influence and recognition on the global stage. The country actively engaged in regional alliances and trade agreements, further solidifying its position as a major economic power.

The removal of Wang and the subsequent events also had a profound impact on China's domestic politics. The Chinese Congress, determined to restore stability and regain the trust of the people, implemented a series of reforms. These reforms aimed to address the grievances of the Muslim population and rebuild the damaged relationship between the government and its citizens.

Efforts were made to repair the damage caused by Wang's ill-advised policies. The new leadership in China focused on regaining the trust of the international community. They implemented policies to attract foreign investments, improve trade relations, and strengthen diplomatic ties. China embarked on a path of economic recovery, gradually rebuilding its global business and regaining its position as a major player in the global economy.

As now, cost of maintaining Tibet and Mongolia were proving to be out of scope for China, the National People's Congress passed a resolution in January 2028, to explore options.

There was a special committee appointed for the same, which was headed by the incumbent President, Deng-Yat-Sen. Deng was the great grandson of Sun-Yat-Sen, the great Chinese leader, who had dreamed for a Chinese republic, way back in 1912.

As for Wang, his removal from office marked the end of his political career. The armed guards stationed at his official residence indicated the seriousness of the situation and the potential threats he faced. His disappearance from public view suggested that he was either in hiding or facing legal consequences for his actions.

What was mine and Yang's contribution in all this?

One may call it by any name, but for us, it was a befitting reply, what China had started.

CHAPTER 23

The Reply

While the Project Wall had resulted in widespread destruction in China, Project Brihadratha had a subtle approach.

It took us over six years to create an environment fit to respond to China's manipulative policies. It was not until December 2027; the response started showing results.

Yang and I were leading two separate teams, within Project Brihadratha. The tool created by Alex in 2018 was further developed in cyber labs. This tool helped both the teams.

Yang was somewhat expert in the Cyber Heist. So, she was tasked for the same. For me, the Cyber world was new, but I had a clear path.

My path required me to supervise Alex, who in turn kept getting information and blueprints of various technologies through his tool.

By 2022, India had started leading the global automotive manufacturing. Big world brands like Jaguar, Land Rover, Mercedes, BMW, Audi, they all shifted their manufacturing to India. Most of the Korean, Japanese and

European automotive brands also, saw India as a big market with cheap labor, so they shifted their manufacturing to India.

While the manufacturing was shifted, China by then had advanced the technology by way of microchips, which they refused to share with India. This is when Alex's tool helped me.

It took us a rogue mail attachment and a wait of few months; the Indian car manufacturers had the latest technology with them. Henceforth, the Indian automotive industry grew leaps and bonds.

Next was the challenge about billions of dollars invested by China in global economies. We had already identified that the Chinese investments were in Oil, Power, Infrastructure, agriculture, aerospace, service industry and technology.

It was time to reply to what China had done for Purshottam Industries, but in a different manner. While China had caused the damage through a manipulated report, we planned to reply with a genuine one.

Mid 2025 onwards, there were large scale shutdowns in oil, power, infrastructure, service and agriculture industries controlled by China. Thanks to the modified tool, which was created by Alex, there were large scale miscalculations in the companies' computer systems and programs, resulting in regular periodic shutdowns.

This badly affected the stock prices, as the Chinese management of these companies appeared sub-standard.

By the beginning of 2026, the stock prices of these companies rock bottomed.

We deliberately did not play with the aerospace industry, as our play could cause large scale loss of life. Still the ticketing systems through service industry were hacked and overnight millions of dollars were siphoned off to different countries.

Yang was supervising the cyber heist for which, another modified version of Alex's tool was used.

By end of 2025, Yang could get the entire details of investments, which China had made in government bonds of various countries.

On July 7th, 2026, there was a devastating Cyber-attack and records of all the investments in global banks vanished. The attack was swift and devastating, causing chaos and panic in the financial world. As the news spread, governments scrambled to contain the damage and investigate the source of the attack.

Yang's plan had been executed with precision, causing billions of dollars disappearing from records and shaking the foundations of the global economy.

Yang and team knew that there were periodic confirmations of investments shared by these banks with the investors. There would be no loss of money, but it would reflect poorly on China's policy of investing their business surplus abroad.

This was the biggest of damage, Yang and team could cause, for which Wang had to pay heavily.

The incident served as a wake-up call for the financial industry, but caused a doom for Wang's political career.

By June 2028, the Chinese declared Tibet and Mongolia as independent states.

While signing the independence treaty, China agreed to the clause of no aggression for the next five years, providing time for Tibet and Mongolia to build their own defense mechanism, for which India had promised to provide all necessary help.

China set Tibet independent during June of 2028. In July, his holiness returned to his homeland from exile to India, after almost 68 years. He had just celebrated his 91st birthday.

China had appointed Dorje Gampo, a prominent Tibetan leader as the governor of Tibet, to form the interim government.

On his return, his holiness discussed with him about his thoughts to form a democratic government. When Dorje agreed, His Holiness acknowledged Dorje as the leader.

Thereon, Dorje approached Indian Government, which agreed to support Tibet, forming a democracy.

The first elections for the democratic government were performed in May 2029 and by June, Dorje was unanimously elected the first prime minister of Tibet, who formed the first democratic government. His holiness remained the supreme leader.

During the Chinese occupation, the Chinese army and police had many Tibetans. Many of them started working for the newly formed Tibetan government. They were now faithful to His Holiness, whom they had termed as traitor till last year.

The last decade saw socio-economic changes in the world. It started with pandemic, which lead to recession, then wars, natural calamities, nations declaring bankruptcies. As the world blamed China, India emerged as a global leader because of its policy 'Vasudhaiva Kutumbakam' which meant, the world is one family. India helped the world during all the above natural and man-made calamities, thus, when India supported the cause of independent Tibet, most of the prominent world leaders came forward in support.

What did India get out of this? The entire 3,500 KM border with China, now had a buffer state in between, which was like an extended family for India. The defense budget for India, saw a drastic reduction, as the constant threat from China was no longer there.

Indians got their free travel permit to their most sacred pilgrimage Kailash through the New Road.

This road promised steady flow of income and supplies to the new Tibet government. The new Tibet government was economically independent because of the tourism it got, all thanks to the Indian leadership.

There was a new destination on the world travelers' map. The enchanting and mesmerizing Tibet, as it was advertised, had much to offer, including peace and spirituality, to the stressed world.

What did I get? A beautiful wife in Yang, close association with His Holiness and Indian government. Of course, additionally I was free now, to be with my remaining birth family.

This story, I could not tell our children. The secret remained with Yang and me.

After our marriage, Yang and I were state guests for a month at historical Pelota palace. Later we were also invited by Prince at his Eddington Estate and above all, by the Indian Prime Minister, who could not be at our wedding.

The Indian Prime Minister, although in his retirement mode after his fourth term election, invited us at his official residence, most importantly, for his blessings.

My parents would have been proud of this invitation. Their contribution, neither I nor anyone in Tibet or India could ever repay.

The new Road to Kailash,
The new road to prosperity.

www.ingramcontent.com/pod-product-compliance
Lightning Source LLC
LaVergne TN
LVHW061609070526
838199LV00078B/7217